I AM THE STORM

THE NIGHT FIRM, 2

KARPOV KINRADE

http://KarpovKinrade.com

Published by Daring Books
~~~~~

First Edition
ISBN-13: 978-1-939559-58-6

~~~~~

To Lind
My soul friend through and through
Let's make worlds
<3 Lux

PREFACE

Before you begin, did you know we also make music? You can listen to a fantasy soundtrack inspired by this series while you read. Check out I AM THE WILD music on iTunes, Apple Music, Spotify, Amazon, Google Play and more.

You can also get all our books and music before anyone else, plus weekly interactive flash fiction. Join our patreon at patreon.com/KarpovKinrade

THE FESTIVAL

When you come out of the storm, you won't be the same person who walked in. That's what this storm's all about. ~Haruki Murakami

"ADAM?" My heart races as my mind tries to process what I'm seeing. My knees dig into the ground, mud from the recent rains soaking into my blue gown. Tears wet my cheeks, and I make no effort to wipe them away.

With shaking legs, I stand to face the man before me.

To stare into the eyes I thought I'd never see again.

The same blue eyes as my own.

My brother cocks his head and smiles crookedly. It's such a familiar gesture that my heart lurches and I take a step forward. Surely, I'm imagining this. Or it's a trick? There's still so much I don't know about the Otherworld. Could someone be impersonating my twin for some cruel reason?

"I know what you're thinking," he says, his long, black

coat whipping in the wind as he runs a hand through his dark hair. "But it really is me. I'm sorry, Evie. Sorry about everything."

I narrow my eyes at him, pieces of the past clicking together into a troubling picture. I've seen this coat before. At Lilith's mansion. While I was shopping one day in town. He's been following me, and I never got a good enough look at his face to realize it was him. All this time I've been seeing my brother in every stranger's face I pass, but I failed to see what was right in front of my eyes.

He reaches for my hand, and as we touch a small jolt of power shoots up my arm. We both widen our eyes in surprise, but we don't let go of each other.

"How?" I ask, my eyes burning with tears. "You were dead. I have your ashes on my fireplace mantle. I mourned for you. I still mourn for you," I say through a heavy wave of emotion, my voice cracking.

He pulls me closer to him, into a hug, his arms wrapping around me, and I lay my head on his chest and hear his heart beat. He feels strong, healthy. The smell of him, of cinnamon and honey catching on the wind, brings me back to childhood memories I had forgotten. Skipping stones on the river. Playing hide and seek by the willow tree. I want to hold onto him forever. To bask in the familiarity of his arms. But then I remember the Memory Catcher.

Mary.

The baby.

And I pull back, shaking, all sense of security shattered. "You're not my brother," I spit, the rage at this deceit boiling up within me. "My brother would never kill anyone. Especially not a child."

He bows his head in the way that always meant he was sorry, and my heart cracks at the familiar gesture. "I had to, Evie," he says, voice soft and yet cold. "The child could not be allowed to grow up."

"What are you talking about?" I ask, tears stinging my eyes. "He was just an innocent baby—"

"No," Adam cuts me off sharply. He speaks quickly, his eyes darting around as if he sees something I do not. "The boy would have killed thousands. On his twentieth birthday, his mother, Mary, is murdered for copulating with a vampire. Murdered by her own fellow humans. Dracula seeks revenge against the killers—destroying them and their families. Anyone who was part of it. But that's not enough for Mary's son. He is the most powerful vampire ever created, and he deems all humans to be treacherous, weak beings. He begins to slaughter them by the hundreds. And those he doesn't kill, he enslaves, like sheep in a pen. His sister tries to stop him. She fails. Then…" He pauses, his voice growing pained as he meets my gaze with bloodshot eyes. "You try to stop him. You fail."

He reaches for my hand, but I pull back, and catch a glimpse of the hurt in his eyes.

"How can you possibly know this?" I ask.

"After I died," he says, "I came back. I don't know how. But when I woke, I was not only healed, but… different. Our father was right, Evie. We do have powers. Mine just took longer to manifest than yours." He sounds excited, like the little boy I remember. The boy who stayed at my side as fever took me after my flashes. "Now I see things," he continues. "Things that have yet to pass. They flow past my eyes like ghosts. Like the future and the present

3

are layered over one another. Both for me to discover. To change for the better."

My jaw clenches. "How could you do it? You...who used to save bees from the hot tub? Who took spiders outside of the house on a napkin?"

He cries then. And despite myself, I wrap my arms around his shoulders, and let his head rest in the crook of my neck.

"Evie," he whimpers, his tears running down my skin. "I see horrible things...things I would not wish upon anyone. They are like nightmares, but I can never wake. The only way to stop them...is to change things." He pulls back to look at me. "The girl, Alina, will have a better life now."

At the mention of Liam's baby, my voice softens. "You fool," I say, shaking my head. "You're my best friend. My twin. I was cut in half without you. Why the fake ashes? The hiding? Why didn't you come to me?"

"I wanted to," he says quickly. "But you had to believe I was dead. Otherwise, you never would have gone to work for the Night Firm. It's...important...what you're doing. What you will do."

"What am I going to do?" I ask.

He sighs. "If I told you, it would never happen."

His words would sound ludicrous if I didn't have visions of my own. If I didn't know things I had no right knowing. I thought my brother had been spared from that fate, but it seems his powers were just biding their time.

"Whose memory was that?" I ask, holding up the Memory Catcher. "Someone watched you through the window."

He nods. "You'll meet them in time. For now, just

remember..." His eyes drift away, landing on the large iron clock on the tower across the town square, then flick back to me. "I will always protect you, no matter what."

Footsteps.

The shuffling of grass.

"There you are," says Sebastian, emerging from behind the trees, carrying two glasses in one hand and a plate piled with treats in the other. "I heard raised voices," he says. "Was someone bothering you?"

My throat clenches, unsure of how to explain this. I turn back to Adam...but he's gone. Vanished as quickly as he appeared. Even his footprints are gone.

My eyes dart to the forest behind me, but there's no sign of my brother. My gut tells me I'll see him again, though. He still has questions to answer.

I turn back to Sebastian, doing my best to look festive despite the worry I feel. "Dracula was here," I say casually. "He wanted to say goodbye and thank me for my help exonerating him." It's not a lie, but it's not the whole truth, either. "Thanks for grabbing the drinks."

Sebastian smiles, his forest green eyes crinkling around the edges. Every time I see him, he steals my breath. You'd think I'd get used to it, to his earthy sexiness, his aristocratic features, his sculpted muscles and tall, lean body. But the earth Druid turned vampire has an animal magnetism that always catches me off guard. Tonight, he's wearing a black leather jacket and black pants with a white tailored tunic that does nothing to diminish his chiseled body. And his pink tie adds a splash of charm to his badass look.

He hands me a plate piled high with food—brightly-colored pastries, éclairs stuffed with chocolate and cream, and an oddly shaped set of donuts with not one but two holes in the center—and one of the drinks. His is red—blood most likely, probably mixed with liquor. Mine is a pretty blue color and I sniff at it. Blueberries and honey.

I take a sip, following Sebastian to a stone table where Elijah, Liam, and Derek are already sitting. Liam lifts a crimson bottle to his baby, and I raise an eyebrow at it as I take a seat across from him.

"Do I want to know why Alina's milk is red?" I ask, shuddering to think of the reason.

He turns to look at me, raising an eyebrow at my muddy and disheveled state but apparently too polite to ask what happened in front of everyone else. When I refuse to answer his unspoken inquiry, his golden eyes narrow momentarily but then goes back to feeding his daughter. "She's half vampire," he says, a flock of auburn hair falling across his forehead. "She needs milk and blood. It's a special mix the Ifrits put together."

"Yum," I say, picking at my own food but not actually eating any.

Liam frowns, then winks, and my body heats up at the memory of his kisses, his hands on me, his passion teasing my senses. Our gazes are locked onto one another's as he admires the sapphire blue gown that hugs my curves and I notice the way the emerald green of his cloak brings out his eyes.

But then the bottle slips from Alina's mouth and a trickle of milky blood stains her pink dress. Liam breaks eye contact with me to tend to her, and I mentally fan myself to cool off from the memories of his body pressed against mine.

Elijah, who sits next to Liam, sips at his blood cocktail and smiles, his silver-white hair swept back in a tie, his top hat covering most of it. He's very dashing in a fine black coat with purple buttons and silver walking stick. "We should buy her red clothing, to hide the blood stains," the air Druid says. "There is much research to be done on raising a hybrid child. We've never had an infant in the family." As if his own comment inspires him, he pulls a book out of his breast pocket and begins to read. I just chuckle and sip at my drink.

"You've hardly touched your food," Sebastian says, with a nudge to my shoulder. "Not to your liking? I can get you something else?"

His attentiveness is touching, and I smile warmly at him while inwardly I wince. "I'm just not very hungry," I say. Seeing my dead brother has sapped my appetite, I want to add. But I can't. Not yet. I trust the Night brothers. I do. They've become my family. But they're lawyers, sworn to uphold the law. And my brother...my brother is a murderer. Who let another man take the fall for his crimes. He may be justified in his actions, or he might be insane. He could be lying, but that seems the least likely. I can't imagine him evil. Not that. Anything but that. But either way, I can't risk the Nights turning him in while I'm figuring out what to do. I already lost my twin once. I won't lose him again.

Derek, sitting on the other side of me, wraps an arm around my shoulders and leans in to kiss my head. "Don't drink too much without food in you. Matilda has tonics ready for us all after tonight, but they take time to work, and you're not going to enjoy the taste."

The charismatic water Druid stands, adjusting his red

7

scarf as he scans the crowds. "I'm off to mingle. Don't get too crazy," he says good-naturedly.

Elijah stands as well, tucking his book into his jacket. "I will join you, brother. Ifi and Elal look like they could use a few drinking companions."

I glance to where he's pointing and see the Ifrits engaged in some kind of elemental drinking game. Derek grins and they leave together, greeting the two men with laughter and back slaps.

Around us the festivities continue. Lily is dancing in her long green gown with other dryads, their movements flowing like leaves in the wind, their true forms flashing in and out as an elf plays a fiddle and a woman who looks part mermaid with scales lining her skin sings a haunting song in a strange language. It's entrancing.

Liam stands with Alina, catching my gaze as he cradles her in his arms. "I'll see you in a bit?" he asks. I nod and he heads to a nearby fire pit where the two gargoyles, Okura and Akuro are perched, talking softy. Well, softly for gargoyles. When Liam reaches them, Okura—the female gargoyle who recently gave birth—pulls her baby out of the pouch so the two newborns can meet. Maybe they'll grow up to be friends. What a lucky childhood Alina will have.

I don't see Matilda, and I wonder briefly if she went home.

Everywhere there is laughter and great anticipation for the night that is to come. Even Lilith is here, her long dark hair slick and shiny as she raises a glass in toast with Kana, the Kitsune who helped us untangle the mysteries surrounding Mary's letters.

Beyond the town center, towering over the stalls and

booths, is the courthouse. Large enough to accommodate dragons and all manner of magical creatures, casting a long shadow across the town with its gothic architecture and grey stonework.

Sebastian and I are the only two left at the table. He is my rock, my foundation in a very strange world, and as he lays a hand on mine, I want to unburden my soul. But instead I pull away, fighting every urge in me to grab onto him and not let go, to hold him close and feel his strength embrace me and erase my fear and worry.

"Everyone looks to be having a wonderful time," I say, hating myself for making small talk with Sebastian of all people.

"That does appear to be the case," he says. "But are you? You seem lost in thought."

Before I can answer, we're interrupted by the arrival of someone intent on saying hello to Sebastian. The newcomer is short, with the upper body of a man—and a very hairy one at that, given that he isn't wearing a shirt and I can still see the thick mat covering his chest and back—and the lower body of a goat. Thankfully, his lower half is covered by a pair of bright purple pants. Sebastian reluctantly engages in conversation with him, and I'm left a bit dumbstruck at the thought that I've just met my first faun.

I say a brief hello and introduce myself, then turn my attention to the party. I search each person, looking for Adam's face in theirs. Looking for my twin. But I know he's gone. The real question is, will he come back?

I'm distracted from thoughts of my brother when someone catches my eye, a beautiful man gliding through the crowd, dressed entirely in black to match his hair.

When he looks my way, I suck in my breath, but I can't turn away. His eyes are dark as night, void of any color. The blackest eyes I've ever seen. And I feel a compulsion I can't explain. I want to be closer to him. To never stop looking at him. To touch him.

He stops to stand in front of a bonfire like a shadow in the flames, mesmerizing. His eyes don't leave mine and his expression is curious. He smiles and I melt inside.

I'm about to stand and walk towards him. Power beyond myself compels me to do so, but then the clock tower clangs loudly, pulling my gaze from his for just a moment. When I look back, the man is gone, and I feel a bitter disappointment.

But his image is seared in my mind, and I kick myself for not bringing my sketchbook tonight. My fingers are itching to draw him. To capture every nuance of his look and expression on paper.

The clock tower continues to chime, and as it does, an overwhelming sense of wrongness takes hold within me. A flash grips me and I stand and follow its pull towards the woods. If I don't move, if I don't obey the compulsion, I will be too sick to function. It has happened before.

Sebastian realizes I'm leaving and grabs my hand. "Are you well?"

But when he sees my face, he frowns and walks away from his conversation with the faun "What's happening?" he asks urgently.

"Something's wrong," I whisper, but it's hard to speak. Hard to form words. I just have to…move. "We have to get out of here."

I pull him with me farther away from the crowd.

The chime ends.

The clock tower explodes.

The force rocks the world beneath my feet, and it's only Sebastian's hold on me that keeps me from collapsing.

From the corner of my eye I see a familiar form surrounded by mist, her eyes sad, her mouth forming my name.

"Eve."

I hear it on the wind. The woman with skin dark as midnight and long silver braids that flow down her back. A silver horn protrudes from her forehead and her large silver eyes watch me with curiosity.

I scream as another flash seizes me and clutch my head as my brain feels as if it's squeezed into a vice. I struggle to focus, my head pounding, bile rising in my throat. And then I smell it. Smoke. Ash. Fire. The rising dust of falling debris. And then I hear the screams.

I turn to look at the town square and I see the flames, the panic, the people struggling to flee the court-yard, a brave few trying to put out the blaze with buckets of water. Smoke billowing everywhere, choking the oxygen out of my lungs. People clearing away rubble. Part of the courthouse has collapsed. The part holding the clock. The source of the explosion. And then I remember.

I look around for Lily. The other Night brothers. I don't see them. I don't see any of them. Panic seizes me. "We need to find your brothers," I yell.

Sebastian's eyes widen. "Let's go," he says, grabbing my hand.

We run towards the direction of the explosion.

I ditch my cloak that's slowing me down, and I try to

pull out whatever power is in me. Can I put out the flames? Help in some way?

Enforcers dressed in black leather organize a group to help put out the fire. It spreads beyond the courthouse, taking down other buildings and many stalls and booths. The Ifrits run in and out of the blaze, pulling people out from under the fallen structures, the flames dripping off them like oil. One of the gargoyles flies large buckets of water from a nearby stream, but it's not enough.

I have to find a way to help.

Anxiety clutches me and I struggle to breathe, to calm my mind. Where are the others? My mind spins with all my deepest fears of losing those I love. If they were near the blast, they could be dead, and I can't handle losing more of my family. Tears burn my eyes and the world feels like it's closing in on me.

Sebastian pauses and glances at me. "Eve?"

But I can't answer him. I'm hyperventilating and I feel dizzy and scared. Like my heart is going to explode.

Sebastian turns to me, putting his hands gently on my face, and I feel a pulse of his earth power flow into me. It's strong, steady, stable, safe.

"Breathe with me," he says, slowing his own breath and encouraging me to do the same.

"Focus on my voice. Focus on my hands on your face."

His hands do feel good, and his voice is deep and rhythmic. Calming.

Finally, I use the tools I have learned over the years to manage my anxiety attacks. I focus on my senses. On identifying and counting things I can see, taste, touch, smell, hear.

And then I feel it.

Welling up within me.

My power.

I close my eyes.

Water. We need water. I put everything I am into that thought, that feeling of covering the earth with water.

Thunder breaks through the sky.

Wind whips around us.

And then...

The rain falls.

I open my eyes, and see Sebastian looking at me in wonder. "Did you do that?" he asks, looking up at the sky.

"I think I did."

His eyes widen in awe, and he caresses my cheek. "You're incredible."

I put my hand on his and smile. "Thank you for helping me. Now, let's go find our family."

The rain continues to pour, a storm building around us. It's not enough to put out the flames entirely, but it's helping.

I call out for Derek, for Liam, for Lily. I look around for Elijah. Where is everyone?

We reach the origin of the explosion, a shattered clock and a crater in the earth, and I suck in a sob. How could anyone survive this? "Liam had Alina with him," I say in despair.

Sebastian squeezes my hand. "He'll protect her. She's part fire Druid, remember. Flames can't hurt them."

I let out my breath. I hadn't thought of that. But..."Falling rubble can," I say.

We jog along the edges of the flames, and I spot a familiar shoe sticking out from part of the collapsed stone structure. "Sebastian!" I scream, pointing.

It's Derek. Face paler than usual. Eyes glazed over. His head and feet the only part of him visible from beneath the rubble. I rush to his side. Start lifting away rocks. One is too heavy for me. My hands are cut and bleeding, but my tears aren't from pain but rather fear. Every moment he's trapped could be a moment too late.

And then a large pillar begins to rise on its own, floating into the air and landing beside me with a hard thud.

I turn to stare at Sebastian, whose forest green eyes are wide with awe. His hands are raised, and I can feel the power emanating from them.

"That was you, wasn't it?" I ask.

He nods.

I stand back as he makes quick work of the rest of the debris, until there's nothing left trapping Derek. I clutch the vampire in my arms. His body is broken, bloodied, and unnaturally still. "No!" I yell.

The flames rage around us, but I don't care. All of my focus is on the unconscious vampire in front of me.

Smoke chokes me as I tilt his head to give him CPR, compressing his chest just as I learned in the classes Adam and I took together when he first got his diagnosis.

I do everything I can, but nothing works. I look to Sebastian, panic on my face. "He's not waking up."

"He needs blood," Sebastian says, kneeling next to me, his hands supporting his brother's head gently.

I nod, knowing what I need to do. I hold up my wrist to Sebastian. "I don't have a knife, can you... "

He knows what I'm asking and takes my wrist into his mouth, biting deeply. The pain only lasts a moment, then a strange pleasure spreads through me. When my blood touches Sebastian's tongue his eyes widen, and he sucks more out before he realizes what he's doing and pulls himself away.

"Eve," he whispers, his pupils dilated, but I can't focus on him right now. I hold my wrist over Derek's mouth, letting my blood drip down his throat.

After a few moments, Derek stirs, his mouth seeking my blood, and he begins to drink.

My head spins and I feel dizzy from blood loss when strong arms pull me away from Derek. Sebastian cradles me in his arms. "You can't give him too much," he says sternly.

I look into his eyes and flick my lids. "You really are always mad at me for something," I say half-jokingly.

Then I hear Derek shift and sit up. He takes my wrist into his hand and licks at the puncture marks there, closing them.

Another explosion rocks the ground, and as terror spreads through the crowd, a figure emerges from the flames of the courthouse.

At first, it looks like an Ifrit, so lit up by fire is he, but as he nears us, I realize who it is, and I swallow a sob and run towards him.

"Liam!"

The fire Druid looks toward me, and I notice the bundle under his cloak, protected from the flames. He pulls out the infant as the fire dies around him. Alina lets out a piercing wail, and I release my breath in relief as I reach them and throw myself into his arms, burying my face in his neck.

He smells of smoke and magick, and my tears burn off

his hot skin like rain hitting scalding pavement. "I feared you were both dead," I say.

His lips find mine and he kisses me deeply, his daughter between us, her tiny hand gripping onto a lock of my hair and tugging as Liam's passion consumes us both.

We are so lost in each other that, at first, I don't hear it, but then, a distant sound intrudes on my consciousness. It's faint but grows in clarity as it draws closer and before long, I recognize it as the beating of wings.

Very large wings.

As I pull away from Liam, I can feel the wind on my face, pulsing in time with the beat of those wings, and as I look up, I see a massive blue dragon descending from above. It is slightly smaller than Dath'Racul, with a sleek, elegant body and deep blue scales reflecting the light like sparkling sapphires. Each of the six living dragons embody an element, I recall, and as this dragon begins to roar, a powerful stream of icy water pours forth from its mouth, striking the flames with a steaming hiss, quenching them more quickly than anything else thus far.

Water falls on us, soaking through our hair and clothes, and from the dying flames and gray smoke, Elijah emerges, silver hair wild in the wind, head bowed, shoulders slumped. A limp body lies in his arms, with skin charred black. And when he comes closer, I see who he's carrying.

Lily.

THE CRIME

You are a storm in transition, even as these words are being written.
  ~Nikita Gill

MY GUT CLENCHES as I run to the wind Druid, the rain I created with my powers growing stronger as emotions flood me, surging my magick. The wind grows fierce and lightning flashes across the sky.

"Is she—?" I'm afraid to say the word as my tears mix with the rain.

"She's alive," Elijah says, "but by a thread. We have to get her home. To her tree."

It takes a moment to see the smallest movement of her chest and I exhale in relief. She's still breathing, but I can barely imagine how. Her beautiful punk hair is singed, and her skin is covered in charred burns that swell with puss. If she were human, I would have no hope, but she's not, so anything is possible. *You'll be fine, I think. You* have to be fine. I cling to that thought as my hand falls to Elijah's back and we walk as quickly as possible to the carriage. Sebastian helps Derek stand up and Liam follows with Alina in his arms, covered by his cloak to protect her from the smoke and rain.

Elijah, Liam, and I squeeze in the back, and while I hold the baby, the fire Druid begins to examine Lily's wounds. Sebastian and Derek sit up front, and Sebastian takes the reins to guide us home.

The horses whinny at the clash of thunder in the sky, and I realize my storm is taking on a life of its own. The question is whether it's doing more harm than good at this point.

I take a breath and try to calm my emotions as the baby in my arms fusses and begins to cry. I hold her closer and rock her, whispering soothing platitudes while I watch Liam.

"How bad is it?" I ask, still marveling that Liam is the healer of the four. I would have pegged the water Druid as a man of medicine, not the fiery hot-headed vampire before me.

He glances up, his expression grim "She needs balms to soothe the burns. Tinctures to facilitate recovery. Even those...may not be enough."

I kiss Alina's head, fighting the tears as I watch one of my closest friends fight for her life.

Sebastian is pushing the horses as fast as he can, but we suddenly grind to a stop after some time of bumping along the dirt road, and Liam and Elijah frown.

"I'll check to see what's going on," I say, taking the baby with me while they stay with Lily.

Outside, other carriages and travelers have halted as

well. It seems the bridge ahead is closed. Derek is still sitting up front, looking a little peaked from being buried under stones. Sebastian is standing in front of an Enforcer, arms crossed over his chest, looking pissed and impatient.

"What's going on?" I ask, walking up to them.

Sebastian gestures to the Enforcer, who's dressed all in black and has a sword hanging from his hip. "He says everyone leaving town has to be searched."

I look to the Enforcer. "Why? Is this because of the explosion?" I ask.

The Enforcer's brown eyes widen, and I wonder what his supernatural race is. He passes as pretty human. At least until I realize he has tiny horns on his forehead that were covered by the hood of his cloak. "I don't know anything about an explosion," he says. "A dragon egg—the dragon egg—has been stolen. By order of the Council of Dragons, no one may leave town without a thorough search."

I place a hand on Sebastian's arm. "We need to allow it so we can get going. Lily's not doing well."

His frown deepens but he nods.

The Enforcer pats Sebastian down, who clenches his jaw and his fists to keep from lashing out at the man doing his job.

When the Enforcer turns to me, I sigh and pass the baby to Sebastian, who cradles her gently as the man pats me down. When he gets to the pockets in my cloak, he pulls out the Memory Catcher Adam left me and my breath hitches.

"What's this?" he asks.

I take it from his hand. "It's for work. We're lawyers," I

say, though technically I'm not quite a lawyer in this world.

Sebastian raises an eyebrow at me, his gaze falling to the crystal in my hand. He'll know it's not one of theirs. He'll wonder why I have it. And I don't have a good answer.

The Enforcer nods. "Right. You defend all the criminals. Like Dracula."

I can tell by his voice that he doesn't approve, and Sebastian's spine stiffens even more. "Everyone deserves a fair trial," he says through his teeth.

The Enforcer doesn't respond. Instead he asks to see the baby.

"Seriously?" I say. "We have a friend in the carriage dying from burns. This baby has just been through hell. We need to get them home. Do you think we're smuggling a dragon egg in her diaper?" I'm about to lose my shit, and the anger triggers heat to grow in my hands. I look down at them and realizing they're hissing in the rain, small tendrils of fire spitting from my fingers.

Sebastian notices and grabs one of them, pulling me closer to him as he holds the baby with the other hand. He leans into me to whisper in my ear, "Stay calm. Take a deep breath."

I do as he says, grateful the Enforcer didn't see me. He's instead peeking into the baby blanket to pat Alina down, who doesn't enjoy the disruption and begins to wail.

"What the hell are you doing to my daughter?" Liam yells, stepping out of the carriage, flames dancing around his hands.

Unlike me, he does nothing to hide his fire or stem his anger.

The Enforcer steps back, putting a hand on the hilt of his sword. "Step back, vampire. Or you'll be arrested. I need to search your carriage."

I realize that this will escalate quickly if Liam doesn't chill. I leave Alina with Sebastian and slip my arm around Liam. "We need to let him, or he won't let us leave and Lily could die," I say softly, as I try to cool his fire with my own powers.

It seems to work, and he simmers down as the Enforcer searches our carriage and pats down the rest of us. When he's done, he sighs, looking more tired than before. "You may go to your home, but just so you know…there will be no leaving the Otherworld for anyone until the egg is found, by order of the Council of Dragons." He pauses, looking at Lily through the carriage window. "I'll provide an escort to help you move along quickly. I hope your friend recovers."

Once we return to the castle, Sebastian takes the baby to her crib while Liam carries Lily to her tree. Elijah and I follow at his heels. Worry for my friend consumes me. We wind through the expansive castle, the grandeur of it lost on me as my focus remains on the shallow breaths that Lily is taking. They seem to be coming further and further apart.

When we finally get to the area where her tree lives, I gasp. The gorgeous blossoms of emerald and crimson, burnt-orange and deep purple, have shriveled, petals dropping to the floor, branches hanging like dead weight from the trunk, a black charred coating covering everything. "What happened to it?" I ask, shocked at the sight.

"Lily and her tree are connected," Liam says. "If she dies, it dies, and vice versa."

He moves forward and the center of the massive trunk opens like a womb. He gently places her into it then steps back.

I sit on my knees and clutch Lily's hand as the trunk begins to close around her. Vines grow over her skin and her eyes flicker open for just a moment. She grips my hand with more strength than I expected. "I saw him," she whispers. "I saw him…"

"Who did you see?" I ask.

But she's already unconscious, the vines spreading over her face. I expect a miracle. To see her charred coating fall away, replaced by fresh skin, but the tree and Lily remain the same. Near death, lifeless, charred. Isn't she supposed to be healing?

Behind me, I hear yelling. Liam's voice. Sharp and mean. "Who else would have done this? Take note of who was injured or almost injured. Our family. My daughter. The Van Helsings want revenge, and this is how they're doing it," he shouts.

"There's no proof," says Elijah, much more calmly but just as loud.

"Then I'll find some," hisses the fire Druid. "Even if I have to wring it from their stupid throats."

I turn away from Lily, my gaze following their voices to the doorway. Liam heads for the exit, but Elijah blocks his path. "You cannot go after them, brother. It will only make things worse." He places a hand on Liam's shoulder.

"Let go of me."

Elijah doesn't. "Use your head for once. If you attack the Van Helsings, you'll end up in jail. How will that help Alina?"

"At least she'll be safe with them gone." Liam raises his hand, flames dancing on his fingers. "But I'm not surprised you'd rather do nothing. You can read books about heroes all you want. But you'll never be one."

Elijah's eyes widen. "I'm not trying to be a—"

"Get out my way!"

Liam shoves his brother aside, and then flies backwards as if hit by a car, slamming into the nearby wall. He stays there, struggling, as if pinned to the stone.

"I won't let you go," says Elijah, his black jacket drifting in a wind I cannot feel.

"Stop," I yell. "Both of you—"

But before I can finish, flames explode from Liam's hand and fly towards his brother. A whip of wind knocks it out of the air. Elijah raises his arm and—

"You will cease this insolence at once," roars Matilda. The small old lady emerges from the doorway, her pinched face filled with fury. She then grabs Liam and Elijah each by the ear, dragging them both down to her height.

"Ouch," squeal both the brothers at once. But they don't fight back. Instead, their faces turn red as they avoid Matilda's disapproving gaze as much as possible.

The wind dies down.

The fire goes out.

Matilda sighs. "I leave you alone for one moment and look what happens. You turn into naughty schoolchildren." She turns to Liam. "Lily needs your healing. Are you going to let her die?"

Liam drops his head. He, at least, has the decency to look ashamed. "No."

"If I let you go, will you behave?" Matilda asks.

"Yes," Liam says gruffly.

"And you?" she asks Elijah.

"I will," he says, still looking away. "You know I will."

She sniffs and lowers her hands, releasing both brothers. "You both need to cool off and clear your heads. And don't you dare use your powers against each other in this house again!"

"Yes, Matilda," they say in unison, rubbing at their ears.

"Now that you're done being idiots," I interject. "Something's wrong. Lily doesn't look any better," I say. "The tree isn't healing."

Liam frowns. "I need milkweed," he says, looking to Matilda.

"We are out," she says. "And nothing will be open with all the chaos. But I know someone who will have some. I'll send a message to have them bring it here as soon as they're able."

I gaze at Liam. "Will Lily be okay?" I ask.

"I won't know until I get her the potion." He sighs. "In the meanwhile, I'll do what I can." He walks back over to the tree and kneels by Lily, placing his hands over her and muttering words I don't understand.

"I'll stay with you," I say, but he shakes his head.

"Go clean up, get some food. You're going to need your strength."

I look down at my mud and ash and water-soaked

dress and realize he's right. I'm a mess. "Okay, but keep me posted?"

He nods. "Matilda. Can you fetch me the salves from my room? Second drawer?"

She nods, walking past Elijah. "You should all clean up," she says to him. "It's going to be a long night."

* * *

ONCE I STRIP my ruined gowned off my bruised and tired body, I do the hand motion to turn on the magical water-fall-like shower and step into the stone enclosure. The hot water soothes my tired muscles and washes away the grime that's caked to my skin and in every crevice of my body.

Closing my eyes, I take a moment to sift through everything that's happened in the last forty-eight hours.

Winning Dracula's case.

Jerry's death.

The emergence of my powers.

That kiss with Liam.

The Night brothers choosing life over suicide when their sire bond was broken.

Liam's child coming to live with us.

My brother returning from the dead.

The explosion.

The injuries.

Lily almost dying.

How can so much happen in such a short time? In any given moment, life can change forever, and you'll never know when that change is about to hit.

How do we get through life with so much uncertainty? So much that's out of our control?

The worst of all these moments flash in my mind and anxiety creeps into me slowly, overtaking my senses. My heart rate increases, and my body begins to shake. I lean against the stone wall and wrap my arms over my chest, then sink to the floor, letting the fear and pain consume me. Sobs wrack my body and everything in me turns dark until I can't see or feel or hear anything.

There's nothing around me but emptiness. Black emptiness. I scream but nothing comes out. Panic seizes me. I try to summon the tools to calm myself, but I can't. It's too much. It's all too much!

But then strong hands grip my shoulders. A soft voice whispers in my ear. My eyes pop open and I look around.

Derek kneels before me, his body glistening with moisture, his short dark hair spiky and wet, his ocean blue eyes pulling me in. The only thing he wears is a linen towel wrapped around his waist. His expression is cautious, but his gaze is warm, and his eyes quickly trail my body then land once again on my face.

"Are you hurt?" he asks.

"I…I don't know—"

He moves towards me, closing the distance between us until our bodies are touching. I suck in a breath as I realize just how little stands between our naked flesh. He seems to have the same realization as evidence of his arousal disturbs his towel.

"I heard you scream," he says.

"I screamed? I don't remember screaming. I was taking a shower and just… thinking about everything that's happened. I guess…I don't know. It all went black."

He raises a hand to cup my face, peering into my eyes. "This is a lot to take in. More than we expected when we hired you. If you regret your choice to work here, to live here, I would understand." He looks sorrowful...almost ashamed.

Is he giving me an out? A way to leave all this behind?

The Night Firm.

The brothers.

I have no life to return to, but I could start a new life, I suppose. Manage a company in New York like I used to, or maybe travel somewhere else. Maybe focus on my art. Everything would be fine. Normal.

But that's a lie.

Even if I wanted to leave the Otherworld behind, it would never leave me. Not if I kept having flashes and abilities beyond my control. Not if I knew my brother was out there somewhere, having visions of his own.

I look Derek in the eyes. My body is practically vibrating, being so near him, and I can't help but close the last breath of space between us, my chest now grazing his ever so slightly. "I don't regret my choices," I say. "But I'm not exactly sure what you thought I was when you hired me." I think of what I did to Jerry. Of what my brother did... my eyes go to the floor, shame and fear warring within me.

"My dad always said to stay in the light," I say. "*In lumen et lumen.* In the light, of the light. What if..." I pause, unsure how to articulate what I've been feeling. "What if he knew that there was something bad in me? Something dark? What if I'm a danger to the firm? To you?" I ask, for the first time expressing the fear that's been building in me since Jerry's death.

Derek blinks, but instead of answering he leans in and claims my lips with his.

The kiss is so unexpected it takes my body a moment to figure out what to do. How to respond. But then I return his passion with my own, knowing it's been building for some time. Through all our long nights preparing for Dracula's defense, through our talks about life and hopes and dreams, through the days of fear that he and his brothers wouldn't be here after the trial.

He pulls me closer to him, shifting his hand to the back of my head, deepening our embrace as I wrap my arms around his waist and splay my hands across the chorded muscles of his naked back. My right palm grazes a wound that hasn't fully healed yet, and though he doesn't flinch, I pull back to look at him, though I regret it the moment our lips are no longer touching. I can still taste him in my mouth. Smokey and minty.

"I've wanted to do that for a long time," he says in a husky voice laced with unspent desire. "Ever since you first walked into that interview."

"Then why didn't you?" I ask softly.

He laughs, and it's a rich, deep sound that reminds me of waves crashing on a shore and the warmth of the sun on my face. The smell of coconut. The taste of salt.

"I…" His words turn into a painful groan.

"You're still hurt," I say, tracing the wound on his back. A pink slash from his shoulder to his hip.

He nods. "It will heal. I would be much worse without your blood flowing through me. Eve…" he whispers my name with reverence and awe, and it melts my insides. "You saved my life."

My lips slightly part, my body mesmerized by his

voice as I feel his wound throbbing beneath my fingers. "You need more blood."

His eyes widen. "We have reserves stashed away. I will be fine."

But I can feel his need as if it's my own and I tilt my head, exposing my neck to him in an unspoken invitation. My breath stills as I wait for him to decide.

And when his lips caress the vein pulsing under my flesh, I sigh in pleasure and close my eyes.

It only hurts a moment, as his teeth sink into me, but then I am flooded with ecstasy so intense my legs go weak. Derek clutches me closer to him, holding me upright as he drinks deeply. His body rock hard and pressing against my belly through his towel.

It takes everything in me not to shed the barrier between us and claim him. I run my fingers along his back, feeling his wound fade away, and—

A knock on the door breaks the spell between us, and Derek pulls back.

"Hurry up in there," yells Sebastian. "We need you in the study. Moira Van Helsing is here."

* * *

DEREK LEAVES THE BATHROOM FIRST. Even after I'm dried and dressed in a cream tunic and dark linen pants, my body still feels swollen with need. But then I recall my recent make-out session with Liam, and I'm not sure how I feel. I want Derek. I want Liam. I want both. So what do I do?

It's not like poly relationships are unheard of, even in my world, but I've never been in a relationship with more than one guy at a time and I don't quite know the rules. And well...I don't really have time to figure them out. Not if Moira's here. Not if Liam is hell-bent on making the Van Helsings pay. This could go south fast.

I pull my wet hair into a bun then head to the library. When I arrive, Elijah offers me a brandy, chocolate covered strawberries, and a plate full of food. I take the silver tray gratefully and sit on the love seat in front of the large hearth, letting the flames pull the chill from my body. Castles are glamorized in modern media, but no one ever tells you how cold they get. The hanging tapestries and rugs aren't just for decor, but for some semblance of insulation.

I notice my plate is piled high with foods rich in iron—beef, beans, dried apricot, and a baked potato—and I glance at Elijah who gives me a slightly rueful smile as he takes a seat next to me.

"If you're going to continue sharing your blood, you need to keep your iron levels up," he says in explanation, slipping his arm around me in protective manner.

At the moment, we're the only ones here, and I take comfort in his presence. Elijah is a quiet man. Thoughtful and careful with his words. A quality I appreciate about him, particularly since it's something I lack in myself.

"Thank you," I say, trying the potato. I don't think I'm hungry, but the moment I start eating I discover I'm ravenous, and I clean my plate in record time. Elijah squeezes my shoulder and nods his head approvingly.

When Derek and Sebastian arrive, Matilda escorts Moira into the study. She's wearing an impeccably tailored dark suit and a crisp blue shirt. Her long blond hair is pulled up in a bun and, as usual, not a hair seems out of place. Despite her outward appearance, one look in her eyes shows how unsettled she is.

Liam is nowhere to be seen. He must still be helping Lily. Good. His presence would only complicate things right now.

Moira looks around nervously, clutching a piece of parchment in her hand.

Sebastian faces her, his face hard. "Did you come to confess?" he asks harshly.

She blanches at his tone. "Confess? Whatever for?"

"For trying to kill us in that explosion!" he says, and I realize though he and Liam butt heads all the time, they're more alike than they want to admit. It actually warms my heart to see Sebastian taking his brother's side, even if it is escalating the situation.

"We didn't try to kill you," says Moira. "We didn't set the fire. Why would we?"

"Let's see..." Elijah says. "Your family hates us, even more so since the death of your despicable brother." His hand tightens around my shoulder with his words, and I shift towards him.

Moira pales. "That's actually why I'm here. Because..." she fidgets with the paper in her hands. "I'm here because we found the letter Jerry received. The one asking him to go to Dracula's house. I...I wanted to show it to you. To prove he wasn't the murderer."

It's my turn to lose all the blood in my face. I already know Jerry wasn't guilty of the murders, but the Night brothers do not. They don't know about Adam. And it sickens me to my stomach.

Derek approaches Moira and takes the letter, scanning it quickly. "How do we know it's not fake?"

"You can keep it," she says quickly. "Have it analyzed. Whatever you want to do. It doesn't change anything, I know. But I just..." she stumbles on her words, then turns to me. "I just wanted someone to know that though Jerry could be an asshole, he wasn't a killer. I don't know who murdered Mary and her child, but it wasn't my brother."

Derek scoffs. "This only proves he wasn't lying about the letter. It doesn't mean he didn't kill them."

There are tears in her eyes, and despite everything, I feel for her. I stand and take the letter from Derek, reading it over. When I'm done, I hand it back to Moira. "I believe you," I say quietly.

Everyone looks surprised.

Especially the Van Helsing. "You...you do?" she asks.

"Yes. If Derek wants to have the letter examined that's fine, but I don't need to. I believe you." Because I know the truth. And because I know how important it is to believe that your own brother, your own flesh and blood, isn't all evil. And though I can't stand Moira, and she put me through hell on the stand during Dracula's trial, I can't let her believe a lie.

She's trying very hard not to cry as she clears her throat. "Thank you, Eve. I...I wasn't expecting that."

I don't know what to say, so I just nod.

She glances down at her shoes, then back up at me again. "I...I know Jerry hurt you. I know he..." she swallows before continuing. "I know he abused you. You weren't the first and probably wouldn't have been the last. We've been covering up his behavior for too long. I'm... I'm so sorry. You didn't deserve that."

Now I'm the one fighting tears. I thought I'd processed my shit with Jerry. With the abuse. With his death. But this kind of healing happens in layers, and there's a shit ton of layers to work through. Just when I think I've got it covered, another wave of emotion hits me. I wonder if I'll ever be rid of that asshole or if he'll always haunt my soul in some way.

"I appreciate that," I say, keeping my voice calm. She's trying, and I don't want to ignore that, but I also can't just let her think a quick 'sorry' is enough. She's part of the problem and she needs to own that. We all have to own our part in the trauma we create for others.

"Listen…Moira, the way you treated me on the stand? The questions you asked me? The victim blaming? Those things weren't okay. You became complicit in his abuse." My words are harsh, but my tone is soft.

She bows her head. "I could say I was just doing my job. It would be the truth."

"Sure," I say, agreeing. "You could say that. But is that the person you really want to be?"

She shakes her head, and when she makes eye contact with me again, the tears she's been holding back flow freely. "You don't understand what it's like to love someone, to be so close to someone who is capable of such acts. It tore my heart in two. Jerry and I were best friends growing up. How could I turn on him? I thought I could help him. Save him from his darkest impulses. He wasn't all bad." She chokes out her last words, and I do something that surprises both of us. I pull her into a hug.

"I do understand," I whisper to her. "I do."

She cries into my shoulder, and the Night brothers watch silently as I console a woman I would have considered my enemy twenty minutes ago.

Maybe she's still my enemy. We will certainly face each

other in court again. Or maybe everyone we meet has a story that would break our hearts, if only we took a moment to hear it. And maybe when we hear those stories, and see those people with new eyes, we will realize none of us are all that different from one another. We all make the best choices we can with what we have. Some of us just have less than others. Some of us have more to lose.

Some of us can't handle the heartbreak again.

Eventually her tears dry, and I walk her out. Something has shifted between us. How long it lasts or what it will look like another day, I have no idea. But for now, Moira and I see each other in a new light, and I grip her hand before she leaves and squeeze it. I don't have words to offer her, but I think we both share the moment just fine in silence.

When I return, Elijah stands and pulls me into his arms.

He isn't the brother I expected to offer comfort, but I accept it. And as we hold each other close, I lose track of time and forget my worries. Even if just for a moment.

* * *

SOME TIME LATER, Liam joins us. No one mentions the visit from Moira. He's too concerned as it is.

"Has the milkweed come?" he asks.

"Not yet," I say. "We're waiting. How's Lily doing?"

"Not well. But no worse." He walks over to a crib in the corner of the library where Alina is sleeping peacefully, and stares down at her, his eyes softening. "Do you think she dreams? Do you think she knows what happened to her mother and brother?"

Guilt floods me at his words. Because I know the truth that he doesn't. And the secret is a cancer eating away at my soul. "I think she feels safe here. She feels safe and happy with you," I say honestly.

He smiles at me, then begins pacing the room as we all wait for the medicine to arrive. I pull out my sketchbook and distract myself with a new drawing. Without thinking, I find myself sketching the mysterious man I saw at the festival. His dark eyes and confident posture. The way he held my gaze with his. The way I felt him calling to me, connecting to me.

I'm so lost in my drawing that when someone knocks on the door, I nearly break my pencil in surprise.

I stick it back into my bag and stand. "Lily's medicine?" I ask. It must be. It's been so long.

Liam dashes to the front door and I follow, hoping desperately that this potion will cure my friend. I can't bear to think of her so injured, burned, after losing her family in a fire. I can only imagine the trauma she's experiencing right now.

Liam swings open the door. "It's about time!" He barks, then stops short when he sees who's there.

Three Enforcers, fully armed, faces hard.

One holds up a parchment. "Liam Night?" he asks.

"Yes," Liam says harshly. "What's going on—"

The Enforcer grabs him, wrapping his wrists in steel carved with magical glyphs. "You're under arrest for arson, public destruction of property, and conspiracy to steal a dragon egg."

THE FIGHT

How do you go back to being strangers with someone who has seen your soul? ~Nikita Gill

THE WARRANT HAS BEEN SIGNED by Dath'Racul so there is little we can do but watch in silence as they drag Liam away. Inside the house, Alina begins to wail as if she knows what is happening with her father. And who's to say she doesn't?

We reconvene in the library, everyone on edge. Matilda rocks the baby, who is inconsolable.

"I'll make sure he gets out on bail as soon as possible," Derek says, sitting at the desk and pulling out a sheath of parchment and a pen.

"They must think he caused the explosion at the festival," Elijah says, scratching his chin. "It did, after all, draw away Ava'Kara, who was needed to put out the flames. The egg was stolen while she was away. That can't be a coincidence."

"That's ridiculous," I say, angry. "Liam would never do that. He and Alina were caught in the blast. He'd never risk her life that way."

"She's part fire Druid," Elijah says. "He would know she'd be fine." I glare at him and he shrugs. "But I don't disagree. I could see Liam setting a fire by accident, if his powers or temper got away from him. But he would never do something so premeditated. It's not who he is. He was clearly framed."

"Who would do that?" I ask. "And why?"

"Someone who wanted that egg," Sebastian says. "And who wanted Liam to take the fall for it. I'll go to the crime scene and see if there are any clues pointing to the real criminal. Or at the very least, anything that could help exonerate Liam."

"I'll go with you," I say. "An extra set of eyes could be helpful."

Sebastian nods in agreement.

"I'll come, too," Derek says, jumping up from behind the desk.

But Matilda tsks us all, setting the sleepy baby back into the crib. "Planning on going now, are you? The streets are swarming with Enforcers who will be none too happy to see you lot. They won't let you near the water dragon's nest."

Derek sighs, looking deflated. "You're right. We won't get anywhere tonight. I'll put in a formal request in the morning."

Matilda nods, her long white braids bobbing on her shoulders. "Good. Then all of you can get some rest. You have a busy day tomorrow and Liam will need you sharp.

I'll wait for the milkweed to arrive, make the potion for Lily, and keep watch over Alina."

Sebastian looks ready to argue, but Matilda stares him down. All four feet of her.

"Don't think that just because you're a big tough guy I can't still take you, my boy. You need blood and sleep, or you'll be no good to Liam or anyone else. This won't be solved in a night."

Sebastian looks sheepishly away, and I almost laugh at how fast this tiny old woman put him in his place.

With minimal grumbling, we all file out of the library and head to our rooms. Elijah, Sebastian, and Derek each nod to me as they pass, and I feel some comfort in knowing we are all in this together. But then I think of Liam, of what his night will look like, and my heart breaks. He doesn't deserve to be in jail. We have to get him out.

When I get back to my room, I notice my window is open. The wind pushes the rain through the curtains and onto the rug, sending a chill through the air despite the blazing fireplace. I wonder if one of the castle ghosts opened it. They live—if live is the right word to describe a ghost?— and work in the castle, but I have never seen them.

My bedroom door closes behind me.

And I feel him there before I turn.

Adam, standing in the corner, next to the urn that I thought held his remains, soaked in rain, and looking as healthy and strong as he did at the festival.

Moon, my feisty black cat, creeps out from under the bed and hisses at the figure by the door, fur spiking on his arched back.

I suck in a breath, my mind whirling. "Is that really you?" I ask. "Or am I dreaming?"

He steps forward. "I'm here," he says, gruff with emotion. "I missed you, Evie."

My voice cracks when I speak again. "I missed you too, Adam. So much."

There is silence between us, and I sink onto my bed, the weariness of the day catching up with me. Moon curls up near my feet, and Adam comes to sit by my side, his hand on mine.

"Did you know the explosion would happen?" I ask.

"Yes," he says.

"Then why not warn me? Or the others? So many were hurt. Some could have died." We still don't know the extent of the damage, but I wouldn't be surprised if there were casualties.

"I made sure you were safe," he says.

"How?" I ask, confused. I didn't see him when the fires started.

"If I hadn't found you, if we hadn't spoken in the forest, Sebastian would have come for you sooner. You would have sat nearer the courthouse, in one of the available seats. You would have been caught in the blast."

I sigh. This is all so confusing. So hard to understand. So hard to believe. All I have is my brother's word that his visions are true. Even if he is seeing them, even if he believes them, that doesn't make them real. Has Adam gone mad? Did dying destroy his mind?

"Why not stop the explosion?" I ask, my voice tired. "My friend was almost killed. Liam's been arrested. If you have this power, this gift, why not stop it from happening?"

39

Adam sighs and squeezes my hand. "I know this is hard for you to understand. And I'm so sorry about Lily and Liam. But things are proceeding as they should. As they must. I couldn't stop the explosion without risking too much."

"What the hell is that supposed to mean?" I ask, angry. "Is this all part of your master plan? Did you cause the fire?" The possibility crashes into me like lightning and I feel sick to my stomach. I think of Moira and her grief at facing the truth of her brother. Her desperate need to exonerate him from whatever crimes she could, even knowing the other awful things he had done. We all wear rose-colored glasses when it comes to our loved ones. We all see what we want to be there, which makes it that much harder to see what actually is there.

Adam puts his arm around me, and I rest my head on his shoulder. "No, Evie. This I did not do." He kisses the top of my head. "But it had to happen. For the sake of the Otherworld. You will understand…in time."

I pull away, facing him, my heart torn in two. "How can I trust you?" I ask. "You murdered a woman and child and—"

"And I told you about it," he says, cutting me off. "I didn't have to show you the Memory Catcher. But I wanted you to know the truth. That's why you can trust me." His blue eyes carry so much grief, so much sadness. "I've never lied to you. And I never will. You can always trust me."

I look away, my emotions all over the place. But he's right, in a twisted way. He's never lied to me in the past. That was our sacred promise to each other. Never to lie.

The promise we never broke. Ever. He didn't have to show me the memory, but he did.

So, if he's not lying...then this is all real...or he believes his own insanity. "Why are you here?" I ask. "Why now?"

"I needed to see you again. To talk to you. To be with you. I've missed you. You're my other half. We are never complete apart. You know this."

Tears leak out of my eyes and I nod. I do know this. We have always been a team.

"But there's more, isn't there?" I ask, sensing it in his voice.

He nods. "There's more. When you find the dragon egg, you'll receive an offer."

"What kind of offer?" I ask,

"To leave the Night Firm," he says. "For... another opportunity. It's important that you accept."

My stomach drops. "Why?"

"That's all I can tell you," he says.

I know from his tone I won't get any more information, so I don't try. I sit with him, safe in the circle of his arm, and I think of all the things we've missed about each other these past months.

"I killed Jerry," I say suddenly, confessing my darkest crime.

"I know," he says softly, tightening his hold on me.

"It's not an easy thing, taking a life."

"It had to be done."

And in a strange way I realize we are connected, even in this. Even in murder, in death, in ending a life.

I marvel at the macabre serendipity of it all. Growing up, Adam and I had always been connected. We shared events in a very twin way. One summer, as children, we were placed in different foster homes. It was the first time we'd ever been apart and the longest three months of my life. It was agony. During that summer, my only consolation was music, and I became obsessed with a country song by Billie Ray Cyrus, Achy Breaky Heart. I listened to that song on repeat the entire summer. Adam and I weren't allowed to call or see each other, and when we finally got a new home together in the fall, we couldn't wait to update each other on our lives. When I told him about the song that got me through his absence, he grinned and showed me the cassette tape he'd been listening to. It was the same song.

This was only one example of so many times our twin powers—as we called them—connected us in shared experiences. When I broke my ankle while on a girl's only field trip, he broke his playing basketball after school with friends. At the same time. Our foster parents were not happy.

And now, we've shared in the act of taking a life. An act that has left a scar of darkness on both of us.

The exhaustion of the last few days settles on me, and I rest my head on my brother's shoulder, my eyelids too heavy to keep open. Adam notices, and guides me gently to my pillow, laying my head down and tucking me in, just like when we were kids. Moon hisses at him and readjusts his position to stay close to me.

"Sleep now, sister," Adam whispers. He kisses my forehead as dreams pull me into their realm.

I'm standing in a dark forest, wind whipping around me. Lightning blazes in the sky and rain pours in torrents through the thick foliage. Thunder rattles the earth, and everything is cloaked in shadow, but I do not feel afraid, only curious.

Then I see him. The darkly beautiful man from the festival, his ebony eyes catching my gaze. Black leather pants hang from his hips and his chest is bare. Celtic tattoos weave across his back and torso, skin glowing in the moonlight. He smiles and I feel the pull of him, the need to be closer to him, to touch him. I can see the magic connecting us, like a smoky wire with a core of light. I walk closer, but he disappears behind a tree. I follow him, but it's like trying to catch the wind in your hands.

I reach a grove of silver flowers and then he is behind me. He grabs my hand and spins me around. His touch electrifies me. His lips move to speak my name, and then I hear another voice, a familiar voice, angry and yelling.

"What is going on?"

I'm pulled out of my dream forcefully and a feeling of whiplash rocks me as my eyes open. I sit up, confused, disoriented, trying to figure out what happened.

Adam is next to me one moment, gone the next, like smoke in the wind. The window slams shut behind him and in the doorway, I see Derek, wild-eyed and angry. He glares at me. "What is the meaning of this?" he asks.

"I can explain," I say, sitting up, my heart beating like a hummingbird against my ribs. What did he hear? What did he see? What does he think he knows?

"Your brother is alive?" he asks. Of course, he would know what Adam looks like. The Night Firm investigated me before hiring me. He knows more about my life than I do, probably.

"Yes," I say, my mouth dry.

"How long have you known?" he asks, storming into the room, peering out the window.

"I just found out. At the festival." I don't want to ask any questions for fear of giving away something he doesn't already know, so I wait.

"He murdered a woman and child..." Derek says. "Mary? And the baby? He's the real killer?"

I pause, considering my options, but I can't outright lie to him, especially when he already knows the truth. I nod, hesitantly.

"My brothers must be told," he says, turning to leave.

I shoot up from the bed, disturbing a sleeping cat in the process, and grab his hand, my actions and voice full of desperate pleading. "No. Not yet. If Liam finds out, he'll kill Adam."

Derek pauses, his face softening just a bit. "I will make sure your brother has a fair trial. I will represent him myself. But justice must be served."

"You can't," I say, my voice cracking. "He...he had a reason for what he did."

"And what reason could possibly justify the murder of a woman in labor and her unborn child?" he asks, his voice heavy with disdain.

And so I tell him all that Adam told me. About the future vision, the child who would have done such evil things. I study him as I speak, but his expression reveals nothing.

"No one can see the future," he says sternly.

"Matilda can," I argue. "She gave me a vision once."

"A vague prophesy," he says. "A glimpse of a possible outcome. Nothing this specific. No one, not even my grandmother, knows what will happen for certain. Not enough to kill others over it."

A sob wells up in my throat. "I can't lose him," I say. "Not again. I can't lose my brother again."

Tears stream down my cheeks and I can't hold it in anymore. The thought of losing Adam after just getting him back is too much to bear. Derek sees the despair on my face and his expression changes. His eyes grow distant. "Sometimes we must sacrifice those we love the most for what is right," he says. He seems to want to say more, but he remains silent.

"Please," I beg. "Don't tell them yet. My brother isn't evil. He can't be evil."

Derek sighs. "They have a right to know. Especially Liam. But… " he walks towards the door. "I will leave this choice to you. If you wish to lie to our family, so be it. I will carry your lie. But just know, it will kill me inside every moment that I do."

He walks out, slamming the door behind him. And I sink to my knees, gutted and heartbroken.

THE PAST

They witnessed her destruction, Then they were left to wonder why, She saw nothing but darkness, Though the stars shone in her eyes.

  ~Supernova by Erin Hanson

DREAMS FLIT in and out of my mind. Sometimes I know I'm asleep and sometimes it feels all too real. I see Adam, his hands covered in blood, crying. Jerry, his dead eyes staring at me, his hand raising to point an accusing finger. And then I see the man from the festival, his energy pulsing and feeling the most alive and real of anything I've ever dreamed. He seems to be reaching for me. Calling for me with a silent voice. But I can never get to him before I wake.

Sunlight streams into my bedroom as my eyes, swollen from tears after my fight with Derek, peel open. I feel like I've got the world's worst hangover, even though I wasn't drinking.

As my blurry vision gains focus, I see someone standing beside my bed holding a tray of food. They're dressed in vibrant green and wearing a red scarf. Liam.

His intense golden eyes study me. "I didn't mean to wake you," he says, a shy smile forming as he puts the platter down on the bedside dresser. "I just wanted you to have some food available when you woke."

I leap out of bed and cut off his flow of words by throwing myself into his arms shouting, "You're back!"

Relief floods me and I can't let go of him. He smells of wood and fire and feels so solid and strong, I could stay in his arms all day.

"I got out on bail," he says, his lips brushing my earlobe.

I finally pull away, though I clutch his hands in mine to keep him close. "Have you seen Lily? Is she okay?"

"She is," he says. "Matilda administered the potion, so Lily will recover. It will just take time. Dryads heal slowly. Trees are not fast at anything."

I nod. "I'm glad she'll be okay. This whole thing has been so awful."

He runs a hand through his red hair, and I notice a pink scar running up his left arm. It looks fresh, puckered, and raw. It wasn't there last night. "What happened?" I ask.

"Just a scratch." He releases my hand to tug his sleeve over the wound. "The Enforcers didn't appreciate my lack of useful information about the crimes in question. They did their level best to loosen my tongue. To no avail, obviously."

He tries to make light of it, but I can see the rage simmering behind his eyes, and I feel it boiling up in me as well. "They tortured you?" I ask through clenched teeth.

47

"I've had worse," he says quietly. Then he drops his head and looks away from me. "I've done worse."

I remember his curse. How his fire raged out of control before he became a vampire. But I get the sense there's more to his words. Other dark deeds in his ancient past.

I'm not naive or stupid. The Night Brothers have made mistakes, done horrible things. I chose to accept that when I chose to stay at this firm and in this family. I'm not here to judge what they've done in the past, but I sure as hell am going to judge what was done to him now. "This has to be illegal," I say, my own temper flaring, the fire in me burning through my skin.

Liam looks down at my hand in surprise as flames dance along my skin and against his. Fortunately, he's immune to the dangers of my fire. Does this mean I'll be immune to his as well, I wonder?

"It is illegal," Liam says, still watching my hand. When the flames die down, he looks up, surprise on his face. "We should test your powers when there's time. They're growing."

"Yes, we should, but right now we need to deal with this mess. If it's illegal to torture, then they need to be brought before a judge."

Liam scoffs. "There hasn't been a new dragon egg since the creation of the Otherworld," he says. "More than a thousand years. Enforcers will do whatever it takes to get it back. And if they break a few rules along the way, who's going to hold them accountable? The dragons?"

I shake my head, disgusted with how some get away with anything while others are held accountable for more than their share. And it all has to do with race, money, and power. Some things are the same everywhere.

I glance at his arm again, at the wound there, and tilt my neck. "If you need blood," I say, the invitation clear.

He runs a finger over my neck, and I can see the desire in his eyes, but he shakes his head and kisses me gently instead. "I've already fed. I just wanted to see you. And to bring you food," he says, gesturing at the platter, which is filled with eggs, cheese and dates, and a goblet of juice.

"I'm starving actually," I say as my stomach rumbles. It's easy to forget to eat when you live with vampires, though they are certainly doing their best to remind me at every turn.

I take the tray to the table in front of the fire and he joins me in the other seat while I eat. "Don't worry," I say. "We have a plan. We'll find out whoever is framing you and—"

"I tortured someone," he says, interrupting me, his gaze lost in the fire, his mind somewhere in the past. The flames dance over his pale skin as he speaks quietly of his past. "Long ago...thirty lashes for the crime they had committed. I...I didn't want to, but it was required of me by my Order."

I reach for his hand, having finished all my food. "What was the crime?" I ask.

"They had forsaken their oath," he says, then glances at me, his eyes glistening with the pain of the memory. "They had given in to the dark Magicks. Used it to kill rather than heal. Thirty lashes," he says, returning his gaze to the fire. "And it was only the start of their punishment."

He pulls his hand from mine and rolls up his sleeve, looking at the red lines that run past his elbow. There is more than one scar and I can only imagine what the rest of him looks like beneath his clothes. "I should have refused," he says, staring at the reminders of his recent torture. "Even if it meant leaving the Druidic Order. I should have refused." He looks away, from the fire, from me, from the memory, maybe. "But I didn't. I followed my orders, even though I was a healer. Even though I was sworn to do no harm."

We are both quiet for some time, and then he turns back to face me, his eyes haunted. "I thought you should know. With…with what's happening between us, whatever it is, I thought you should know the truth of me."

"Oh, Liam," I say, touching his face gently, searching his eyes. I see the compassion in him. The healer beneath the hothead. "I do know the truth of you," I say. "And your past deeds are a part of you, but they are not the whole of you. They are not the complete truth. Believing they define you is the true lie."

For a moment, as I study his beautiful face, his soulful eyes, I wonder if maybe I could tell him about Adam. Maybe he wouldn't react in haste. Maybe…

A polite knock at the door startles me out of my thoughts. We both turn to see Elijah clearing his throat. "Apologies for interrupting. It's time to investigate the crime scene," he says to me. "That is, if you still wish to go."

I nod. "I'll be right down."

Elijah looks at his brother and smiles warmly. "It's good to have you home," he says, before closing the door behind him.

As we get downstairs, we hear arguing coming from

the library. It seems every five minutes at least two of the Night brothers are going at it.

Sebastian's voice carries the loudest. "What do you mean you're not going?" he demands.

"I mean, I have a case to prepare," Derek says coldly. "Even if we find the egg, it won't be enough to exonerate Liam. They'll think he's just giving it back to avoid more punishment. We'll need to prove his innocence to the jury. Show he had no motive. Redirect blame onto other parties—"

"And we will," Sebastian says, irritably. "But in the meantime, I need you by my side. Ava'Kara likes you. You two share elemental magic. Who else am I supposed to bring to the lair of the water dragon? The fire Druid?"

We walk in and Derek glances at me, then looks away sharply. "You'll have Eve."

"Get your head out of your ass," Sebastian says. "We're going." He looks at me, frowning. "Ready?"

"Yes," I say.

We walk towards the door, Liam joining us, when Elijah grabs him by the shoulders. "Hold on there, brother. Sebastian's right. You can't go near the water dragon right now. If she sees you, it will just make things more difficult. Especially for you."

Liam's temper flares instantly. "So, what am I supposed to do?" he demands. "Sit on my thumbs while you read?"

Elijah shrugs. "If you insist. But no, I was thinking we should come up with other leads. Discuss past enemies of yours. Make a list of who else we could investigate to create reasonable doubt."

"That's a good idea," I say, brushing my hand along Liam's arm.

"Whoever murdered Mary is behind this," Liam growls, and my heart sinks at his words and at his anger.

"But that was Jerry," Sebastian says.

"You saw the note," Liam says. "It might not have been him. He wasn't lying about the note and he might not have been lying about the murders. Which means the real killer could still be out there. And now they might be after Mary's remaining baby. After my baby."

I put a hand on him to calm him. "I don't think it's the same person," I say. And it's true. I don't think Adam is behind this.

Derek looks at me, then at Liam, and his face twists in disgust. He leaves the room and heads to the carriage without another word while Liam seethes with rage. It's clear that while he may have felt sorry for hurting someone in the past, he will not feel bad for punishing whoever killed Mary and her baby. I can see in his eyes there's no room for compassion. Liam will be the death of my brother, and my heart breaks all over again. One day soon, I will lose one of the men I love. I just don't know which.

THE DRAGON

No one but Night, with tears on her dark face, watches beside me in this windy place. ~Edna St. Vincent Millay

WE TRAVEL by carriage to the water dragon's lair. While Derek drives, Sebastian and I sit in the back as we bump along a winding road. As the castle fades from sight, and we drive past homes that have seen better days, the earth Druid raises an eyebrow and leans closer to me. "What's going on between you and Derek?" he asks.

"You noticed that, huh?" I study my hands and fidget with invisible lint on my pants.

"It would have been hard not to," he says, softly.

Shit. I don't want to lie to anyone else. "I...I can't tell you. It's... "

"Between you and him," Sebastian says. "I understand. I just hope he didn't hurt you."

I realize he means romantically, like a lover's quarrel and I shake my head. "No, it's nothing like that. He didn't hurt me. If anything, I'm hurting him." I pause, leaning into Sebastian's shoulder as his arm wraps around me. I savor the comfort of him—the warmth of his body, the subtle scent he gives off—as I say what I can without betraying Adam.

"I don't want to lie to you," I begin. "But I can't tell you the whole truth either. Not yet." I sigh, twisting the edge of my shirt in my hands. "There's a choice I have to make. Only...I don't know how to make it. I don't know what the right course of action is. People always talk about things like it's so easy to know what to do, that the hard part is doing it." I look up at his forest green eyes. "I think it's the opposite. It's easy doing the right thing. The hard part is knowing what the right thing is. That's what's paralyzing."

He nods in understanding and squeezes my shoulders. "Sometimes there is no right choice, only the choice you will regret the least." He pauses, looking out the window of the carriage. "Take your time," he says, returning his emerald gaze to me. "I'll be here to talk whenever you're ready."

A flood of emotion crashes through me and I lift my hand to his face, cupping his strong square jawline. "Thank you, Sebastian," I say. "I know you'll always be by my side. I know you'll protect me."

He frowns, placing his hand over mine. "I haven't always protected those I love."

The word love strikes me, and in a moment of abandon I erase the little distance that remains between us and press my lips to his.

He is the first Night brother I met. The first I felt this strange and unyielding attraction to. The first I craved, and yet we have danced around each other, never quite meeting in the same place. Until now.

Sebastian moans against my lips, his body tensing and then he pulls me into his lap and I sigh at the closeness, at the pleasure that cascades through me as our kiss deepens and his tongue explores mine, his teeth tugging at my lips, his fingers pressing into my back, digging into my flesh, his body pulsing with the need I also feel.

When the carriage stops, I sit back, surprised by the intensity of our connection. His eyes are dilated, and his body is needy with desire. I ease off his lap, shaking from the euphoria of finally feeling him so close, and yet craving more. Craving it all.

He kisses me once more and glides his hand through my long hair. "You are more than I ever could have hoped for," he says.

Then Sebastian exits the carriage and I follow him, tugging at my clothing to right them.

We've arrived at a pool of sapphire water hidden in a cove. Several waterfalls pour into it from steep cliffs above, and as we step out of the carriage my feet squish into bright emerald moss that lines the shore. Near one of the waterfalls, a mermaid rests languidly on a partially submerged boulder, her pink and purple fins glistening in the light of the Dragon's Breath.

Derek hails her from the shore. "Greetings, Mira. We are here to examine the nesting site of the egg. We have the necessary documents, of course." Derek pulls out a parchment to show her.

"You are expected," Mira says over the waters without looking at the paper. "You may enter. Do you need accommodations for entry? Or would you prefer to do it yourself? We have heard your abilities have returned, Water Druid."

"Word spreads fast around here," I mutter, and Sebastian just grunts in dry amusement.

"I will make my own path," Derek says and then raises his arms. As he does, the water before us parts, making a path of dry land to the center waterfall.

Sebastian and I follow Derek. I marvel at the walls of water that have formed on both sides of us. Fish and other larger creatures I can't see clearly still swim within them. I take a cautious step closer to Derek, not wanting to be left behind to face whatever is submerged beneath these waters.

When we reach the waterfall, Sebastian takes my hand. "Don't worry. You won't drown."

"I wasn't worried, until you said that," I say with a snort.

Derek enters the waterfall first and it parts for him. Sebastian and I step through next, then drop into a dark stone hole slick with water and slime.

We slide down the hole like the world's most terrifying water slide, and Sebastian catches me in his arms when we land in a bubble of air made by Derek. Around us looms an underground city full of wonders that my mind can scarcely comprehend. An underground castle made of sparking stone and coral stands tall, a plethora of plant life in bright colors dotting the landscape around it. Merpeople form an impromptu line to either side of us as we float to the entrance of the castle. Some are swimming, some are riding what look like giant sea horses. Derek uses his magic to guide us within the walls of the fortress, where we no longer need the air bubble. I hear a slight pop as it dissipates around us and the thick humid scent of moss fills my nostrils. We land gently on our feet and walk to a grand door guarded by an Enforcer dressed in the customary black.

"We're here to examine the nest." Derek once again holds up the signed parchment. "We've already requested permission."

The Enforcer—who appears mostly human despite his fury tail and ears—takes the paper and examines it, turns it over a few times as if some magical words might appear —which, given where we are, might be legit— then nods. He's a beast of few words as he escorts us through the door and down a long hall lined with more Enforcers heavily armed and on alert. We get to large stone doors that require massive strength or magic to open. The Enforcer pulls out a clear crystal and sticks it into the center, and the doors part, stone grinding against stone, shaking the floor beneath us.

"It would take someone highly skilled and connected to infiltrate a place like this," Sebastian says.

I look at the Enforcer, who stands by the door as guard with the other two already there. "How many people have stones that can open this room?" I ask.

He looks down at me with an unreadable expression. "Only the Elite and the Dragon Queen herself. Five in total."

"We should look into who had access," I whisper to Sebastian, "and see if any of those crystals went missing."

He nods as we walk into the nest, and I stop and sweep my gaze over the incredible display of wealth before us. We are in a cave full of blue crystals that shimmer with their own internal light, casting fractal reflections off the gems and gold piled high everywhere. I shake my head, wondering why this level of wealth would be hoarded rather than used to enrich the lives of those in the Otherworld.

Not everyone here lives in mansions and castles. While on our drives through the countryside, I've seen those who live in squalor and poverty. Those who have lost all they have to fires or feuds with other supernatural clans. The wealth on display before me could help so many.

But that's not why I'm here, I remind myself, refocusing my attention on any clues we might discover. I walk to the nearest wall and hold out my hand to see if I can sense anything with my powers. Since I have no real idea what I can do, I'm mostly winging it, but I do feel the thrum of the magic that lives in this whole place. Across parts of the stone wall are black marks that look like deep scars in the rock.

At the end of the cave, much to my surprise, a pair of burning Ifrit are leaning over something on the ground. Flames rise from their reddened skin as from wood in a fire pit, casting everything around them in an orange glow. Looking at them, you'd think they'd smell of burning flesh—which isn't a great scent. But it's more a smoky smell, like the remnants of a campfire.

"Ifi? Elal?" I walk over to them and they turn, smiling, and dim their fires until they look almost human. Ifi, the smaller one, is dressed in a white lab coat and Elal, the taller and more musical of the two, is wearing a dark cloak and slacks underneath. They both have burnt orange-red skin and red hair that looks impossible to tame. Their eyes glow like mini suns and it's almost hard to maintain eye contact with them for long with how intense their gazes are. "What are you two doing here?"

Ifi glances at his feet and I see the body on the ground.

"Ah," I say, solemnly. "I didn't realize there were casualties."

Ifi walks over and hugs me. Fortunately, he's not covered in body goo this time. "Girlfriend, there are always casualties in life. And this is a mess of one. I know I say this a lot, but I really mean it. It has been a day. Has it not, Elal?"

Elal joins his lover and nods. "Ifi isn't exaggerating this time. It has, indeed, been a day."

Then Ifi frowns, gripping my arms. "We heard about Liam and are so sorry. How's that sweet little girl doing?" he asks.

Ifi and Elal took care of Alina after Mary's death, so of course it makes sense they would have a bond with her. "She's well. She wasn't hurt in the explosion. Seems she got her dad's penchant for fire-immunity," I say. "But I'm sure she misses you. You should come for a visit soon."

Ifi claps his hands in delight. "Yes, please and thank you." He looks to Elal. "I think we need a baby, lover. I miss Alina, don't you?"

Elal puts an arm over Ifi's shoulder. "I do miss her. And maybe it is time to expand our family."

I'm dying to ask what the process is for two gay Ifrits to have a child in the Otherworld, but one: that seems rude and inappropriate, and two: I just now notice the details of the body at their feet and I have so. Many. Questions.

The Enforcer is more creature than person. Very whip-like with hair made of tiny serpents, now dead, and a body that ends not in feet but in a long snake form wrapped in a black Enforcer uniform. Their eyes are also blindfolded. "Why are their eyes covered?" I ask.

"My dear, that is a basilisk," Ifi says. "One look into her eyes would paralyze you."

"So, she wore this while alive?"

"Yes," Elal says. "Else she would make a very ineffective guard, paralyzing everyone she saw."

Sebastian joins us, laying a hand on my back. "I've battled a rogue basilisk in the past. They are not ones to trifle with."

"How could she see anything if she was always blindfolded?"

"Their other senses are extremely honed," Elal says. "She was especially gifted. Top of her class at the academy. Her name was Ethne Brinn. 6'7", single, parents deceased."

Sebastian crouches to examine the body more closely. "Cause of death?"

"Stabbed in the bloody chest," Ifi says dramatically. "And the skin around the puncture wound is black, indicating it's decaying faster than the rest of the body."

"Like those black marks on the wall," I say, noting the similarities.

Sebastian nods. "This was dark magic. Not something you see often anymore." He glances at the marks on the wall and frowns. "Where are the other victims?"

"There are no other victims," Elal says. "Just her."

"Only one person was left to guard the egg?" Sebastian says, disbelievingly. "That seems highly reckless."

Elal nods. "There are usually a few more guards from the Elite, but the attack happened during a shift change, apparently."

Derek pauses his examination of the nest to listen to our conversation, though he doesn't join us. He's still pissed, clearly. I don't blame him though.

"This was well-planned," I say, thinking things through.

Sebastian nods. "At first I thought whoever did this took advantage of the explosion at the courthouse. A bit coincidental but possible. But this happening during a shift change makes that unlikely. The timing is too perfect. The crimes must be related."

"These are dark times," says Ifi, shivering. "Earthquakes. Fires. Storms. Missing corpses."

"Wait, what? Corpses have gone missing?" I ask.

Elal nods. "Someone has been breaking into the morgue and stealing the bodies. Particularly, rare races."

"Aren't the morgue and cemetery guarded?" I ask, remembering that the two gargoyles, Okura and Akuro, were powerful deterrents to mischief when I first visited there.

"Normally, yes," Elal says, crossing his muscled arms over his chest. "But they've been on maternity leave since their baby was born. Newborn gargoyles have become rare in recent years, so they're keeping to themselves more than usual."

"Indeed," Ifi says. "I was surprised to see them at the Midwinter Festival. But, oh, that baby. So cute." The Ifrit looks up at his lover with large glowing eyes, and I smile. One way or another, those two are getting a baby sooner than later if Ifi has any say about it.

Sebastian frowns. "Rare bodies being stolen? You don't think it could be..."

Ifi nods. "It very well could be. But there's no way to tell."

"The body is ready," Elal says, interrupting the conversation. "We should extract her dying wish."

"Right, yes. Of course," Ifi says. He kneels at the head of the basilisk and lays his hands on her, then closes his eyes.

Sebastian and I back up, but Elal stays by his side.

Fire erupts from him and spreads flames all around them as Ifi chants in an ancient language. When the flames die down, the body is aglow with some kind of preternatural power.

The basilisk rises from the ground, turning her head to face us. Her voice is more snake than human, a hiss on the wind that loosely forms the words. "Do not ssssearch for the egg. Do not sssssearch."

With that, her body collapses back to the floor and we all let out a collective breath.

"Well," Says Ifi. "That's not what I expected. It's more like a message than a dying wish."

"Can last wishes be tampered with?" I ask. "Like how certain paranormals can mess with Memory Catchers."

Elal shrugs. "It has never been done to my knowledge. But that does not mean a very powerful being couldn't have found a way to do it."

"There's another explanation," Derek says, finally joining us and speaking for the first time since we entered the cave. "She was in on it. She helped steal the egg."

"But… she was killed," I say.

"Her partner could have betrayed her in order to cover their tracks and eliminate witnesses. It's happened before," he says. "Not everyone is as they seem." He looks at us. "Think about it. Why were her eyes still covered? If someone was attacking, she would have uncovered them. They are her greatest weapons, after all. And how would anyone have gotten in here without a crystal to open the cave? It hasn't been damaged or tampered with in any other way that I can see. Her being a party to the crime is the only explanation I can see that makes sense."

His logic is sound. "But, why? Why would she do this?"

Derek shrugs. "Why does anyone commit a crime?" he asks. "All criminals have their justifications that they think exonerate them from their own evil."

I wonder if he is still talking about the basilisk or my brother. I try to brush the thoughts aside. "If she was in on it, why frame Liam? And what was she intending to do with the egg?

Before Derek can respond, the Enforcer who escorted us here returns, speaking promptly. "The Great Ava'Kara wishes to speak with you," he says.

Sebastian, Derek and I turn to follow him, but the Enforcer pauses. "Only the Water Druid and the woman," he says.

Sebastian shrugs. "You go ahead. I'll keep looking around here, and I'll dig into the basilisk's past a bit. Maybe there will be a lead."

Derek and I follow the guard, and when we are out of earshot of the others, I whisper to him. "How long will you keep ignoring me?" I ask.

He smiles, and it would almost look sincere if not for his eyes. "Is this what you want? Me to pretend? While my brother is facing an eternity in prison or worse? These may be his last days of freedom and I'm lying to him for you." He spits out the words like acid, and I recoil from the anger.

"I...I'm sorry," I say sincerely. "I shouldn't have asked you to lie. You..." I force myself to say the words I know I must. The words that will damn my own brother while giving his brother answers. "You can tell him the truth if you wish. I won't have you hurting yourself for me."

Derek freezes, visibly blanching at my words as if he's seen a ghost.

"What's wrong?" I ask.

"Just...I've heard those words before. Long ago." His voice softens into memory. "So very long ago."

"Proceed inside," the guard says, interrupting us once again and pointing us through a door just ahead.

We walk into a great hall with a throne in the center made of seashells and gemstones. Behind the throne is a waterfall that opens up to a large body of water somehow magicked not to enter the throne room itself. Through the water I see blue scales, the giant body of a dragon swimming underwater, like a great sea serpent of legends.

The dragon approaches the waterfall and as she moves through it, her body begins to glow a blinding blue. She shrinks, the closer she gets to the throne, until she steps out of the water not as a dragon, but as a beautiful woman where the dragon had just been.

She is naked and her body shimmers a striking blue. Her hair is white and flows around her, long and wild. She stretches her dragon wings to fullness, revealing their width and beauty, then they settle at her back, becoming a cloak around her. Tiny white horns dot her forehead, and her blue eyes are large—larger than any human—and still very dragon-like.

"Good to see you again, Son of Water," she says in a silky voice. She takes a seat at her throne, crossing her long legs. "I received your petition to speak with me. You have come to argue the innocence of your brother." It's not a question, but Derek nods.

"Approach," she says.

We walk forward until we are about five feet from her throne.

"Speak," she commands.

"Liam was not part of this attack," Derek says, bluntly. "But we need your help to prove it."

She cocks her head. "The Son of Fire was seen exiting the explosion unharmed. He's known for his temper. And the event was clearly a distraction for someone to steal my egg. Why should I believe he wasn't part of this conspiracy? Many would pay well for the egg of a dragon."

"We have no need of money," Derek says.

She leans forward. "Money is not the most valuable currency, as I am sure you are aware."

"Kara, you know our family. You know this is not what we trade in nor is it how we work."

Her eyes narrow. "I know many things," she says. "But foremost I know my egg is missing and there are many who would like to see the Eternal Dragons fall. I can no longer be sure who are enemies and who are friends. Someone has betrayed us, and someone will pay."

She closes her eyes for a long moment, then opens them again, the reptilian movement of them a bit unnerving on her nearly human looking face.

"While I have no doubt about that, it just isn't possible that Liam was behind this," I say, and they both turn to look at me.

"Ah, the human who is not human has found her

voice," the dragon says. "Tell me, Eve Oliver, why isn't this possible?"

"This took planning. Time. Liam—and all of us—have been wrapped up in a case that only recently resolved, resulting in the reemergence of his powers. In fact, they came back that very night. And they wouldn't have come back had we not won the case. Whoever planned this wouldn't have relied on something as untenable as Liam getting his powers back. Things could have easily gone the other way and the plan would have been ruined as a result."

The dragon stares at me a long time, and I wait, knowing that sometimes it's better to shut up and let the other person make up their own mind. If I keep talking, I might inadvertently say something that pushes them in the other direction.

"Tell me, Eve," she says softly, "Do you know what you truly are?"

I sigh. "I don't. Everyone keeps asking me and I don't know."

"Approach," the dragon says once again, and this time she means that I should come up to her throne.

I glance at Derek, but he nods, so I move close enough to her that she can reach out and slide a finger along my forehead, closing her eyes as her body begins to glow blue again. A wisp of power washes through me, disappearing as soon as she pulls her hand away.

"Interesting," she says. "You are most interesting. I can see why so many are fascinated with you."

"Can you… can you tell what I am?" I ask, desperate to know myself better.

But she doesn't answer my question. Instead, she asks another. "Why do you work for the Night brothers?"

This isn't a question that I expect, and it throws me off. I flounder for an answer and then give up, trying instead to bring the conversation back to Liam. "Please can you help us find the truth?"

"Silence, girl. I am asking the questions. And you have yet to answer mine."

So much for avoiding the issue. "I started working for them because I needed a job and a new life after my twin brother killed himself. I stayed with them because they have become my family. Maybe dysfunctional at times, and full of conflict, but family, nonetheless. I would never abandon them, which is why it's so important to me to find out the truth and exonerate Liam. He is a father now. He is my friend, and something more. He is needed in our family."

She leans back, studying us, twirling a gold ring on her middle finger. After a moment, she pulls the ring off and gestures for me to come forward. "Take this," she says. "It is my mark. And it will help you in your investigation. Use it to travel through the Otherworld unhindered." She holds out her ring to me and I accept it, studying the sapphire stone and signet within.

She looks to Derek. "I am surprised you are so convinced of your brother's innocence, Son of Water. You know better than most, not all Druids follow their own code."

Derek frowns and the dragon flicks her wrist dismissively. "You may leave but know this. We are the Eternal Dragons of the Otherworld. This will not be like any other trial. Someone will pay, and if my egg isn't returned to me by the end of this, that someone will be Liam."

* * *

WE ARE ESCORTED out of the throne room and back to the nesting cave where Sebastian is still investigating. While we walk, I reach for Derek. "What did she mean? About Druids not following their own code?" I ask.

Derek frowns and caresses my hand with more tenderness than he's shown since finding out about Adam. "It means I too have secrets... secrets I must hold close," he says with a sigh. "And given that, I will keep your secret for now. Perhaps we are more similar than I wanted to accept."

His words don't sit well with me, but it's clear he doesn't want to talk more about it, and his words at least ease my fears of losing my brother, for the time being.

When we get back to the cave, Sebastian is finishing up a conversation with another Enforcer. "How did it go?" he asks when the Enforcer leaves.

I hold up the dragon ring. "We have some privilege, but she's not convinced of Liam's innocence. And she seems weirdly interested in me," I say.

Sebastian frowns. "As word of your powers and unknown origin spreads, more and more will become intrigued. That worries me."

Derek puts an arm around my shoulder. "We'll keep her safe, if it comes to that."

Sebastian nods, his eyes flicking to my mine with unspoken questions about the change in Derek.

"I'll keep myself safe, thank you very much," I say,

smiling. "Just as I did before. Now...did you find out anything about the basilisk?" I ask.

"She was well-respected," Sebastian says. "No known enemies. A rule-follower to the letter. Not much of a personal life that anyone can attest to. There's not much to go on."

"That's disappointing," I say, and I notice the body is gone along with the Ifrits.

"There is one more thing," Sebastian says. "None of the crystals that open this cave are missing. That further reinforces our theory that she was in on it."

"We've found all we're going to find here," Derek says. "It's time to head back and regroup, see if Elijah and Liam made any progress."

Once in the carriage, Sebastian by my side and Derek driving, the earth Druid leans into me. "You two worked things out?"

I shrug. "For now. It's...complicated."

And then I turn to him with a question I've had for some time. "Is this...is this okay?"

"Is what okay?" he asks.

"Well, I've...I've got this thing..." I say, flailing my hands as if that adds meaning to what I'm trying to convey, "with all of you. I mean. I haven't like, gone all the way with anyone, but..." I blush and don't know how to continue, but Sebastian spares me with a hand on mine.

"Eve, this isn't the human world. We don't do things the same way. There aren't the same taboos. This isn't the first time we have all been in love with the same woman, though it might very well be the last."

I swallow through a dry throat, my eyes widening. "In love?"

He nods. "It's maybe too soon, I realize, to talk about that, but you must know that you have done something to all of us. You have brought light back into our world. Hope. A reason to live. What is love if not that?" He brushes wisps of hair from my forehead, his gaze penetrating mine. "There is no jealously, only a desire to be with you, to make you happy, to protect you. And there is no pressure, not from any of us. Trust your feelings. We aren't going anywhere."

My heart expands with his words, and the fear I hadn't fully articulated turns to joy. I don't have to choose one of them! I can actually have them all. Because in truth, I can't imagine my world without any of them, and though it's taking me time to get there, I know the Night brothers are my future.

I just hope his words are true, that none of them are going anywhere. I hope we can, in fact, prove Liam's innocence before the worst can happen.

My mind wanders back to our investigation in the cave and I recall a conversation that never finished. "Who do you think is stealing the corpses?" I ask. "You mentioned someone to the Ifrits."

"He calls himself the Collector. He procures rare artifacts and sells most of them to the highest bidder in secret auctions. It's well known his means of acquiring said artifacts are rarely legal."

"Let me guess. He's rich and powerful and so he's untouchable."

"Don't forget well-connected," Sebastian says bitterly.

"It's the same in the mundane world," I say. "The powerful do as they please and they rarely even get a slap on the wrist." I shake my head, disgusted with the imbalance that exists everywhere, even in other worlds. "Do you think he stole the egg? That would be quite the item to add to his collection."

"It's possible," Sebastian says. "But this feels too risky, even for him. Still, it's worth investigating. If he didn't steal it, he might know something about who did. He has eyes and ears everywhere. In the highest levels of government and law, and in the lowest alleys."

When we arrive at the castle, we find Liam and Elijah are in the library talking.

"We have a lead," I say, grabbing an apple from a fruit platter someone has taken to leaving out for me. "The Collector."

I bite into the crunchy sweetness as Elijah raises an eyebrow curiously. "We have one as well, but it's not good," he says.

"Who?" asks Sebastian, taking a seat by my side.

"The Beggar Queen," he says, closing a book on his lap. "She disagrees with the policies put in place in the last few centuries by the Council of Dragons and could have taken the egg for leverage in those discussions."

"Or out of spite," Liam says, folding his arms over his chest and staring into the fire.

Elijah stands and paces the room. "The problem is—"

"She won't meet with us," Sebastian says, finishing his brother's sentence as he looks to me. "We've tried before."

"It won't be easy to reach the Collector either," Elijah says. "He doesn't exactly deal with lawyers. Well, not honest ones, anyways."

We all take seats and continue discussing possible avenues to reach our two biggest leads. I don't have a lot to add to the conversation, given my newness in this world, so I listen and pull out my sketchbook to draw. I flip open to the drawing I've been working on of the mysterious man who keeps finding his way into my dreams. I add some details to his eyes and blend the shadows around him. There is something...familiar... about his features, I realize. As if I should know who he is.

As I work to make the sketch more detailed, Liam glances at the drawing, and his expression hardens. "What is this?" he asks.

I'm surprised by his intensity. "It's just someone I saw," I say. "You're not jealous, are you? It's just—"

"Where?" he asks. "Where did you see him?" His voice is urgent and angry. This is more than jealousy. Something is wrong.

"At the Midwinter Festival," I answer. "Before the explosion. Why? Who is this?" I ask, holding up the drawing so they can all see better.

The other three brothers lean in, their eyes going wide at the picture.

"It can't be him," Derek says, his eyes haunted. "It's impossible."

"Look at the drawing," Liam says, taking the sketchbook from me to study more closely. "She saw him. He's back."

Sebastian pales, his jaw hardening, but he says nothing.

"Who?" I ask. "Tell me." Lily's words come back to me then. She said she saw him. Is this who she meant?

Liam's rage turns to ice, his glare glacier as he studies me. "Our brother."

THE BROTHER

When you light a candle, you also cast a shadow. ~Ursula K. Le Guin

"BROTHER?" I ask, confused.

Sebastian lowers his head, still silent. Derek shifts in his seat. Liam begins pacing again, and Elijah just looks like he wishes he were reading—or doing literally anything else—rather than having this conversation.

Finally, Derek clears his throat. "There are five us. Five Night brothers, not four. Who you've drawn," he says, pointing to my sketch, "...that's the fifth and youngest of us. The likeness is unmistakable."

My jaw drops open in shock and I snap it closed. "Why...how did I not know this? Why didn't you tell me?"

"Because he betrayed our Order," Sebastian says with clenched teeth. "Long ago, before we became vampires, before we became cursed, our brother betrayed the

Druidic order. In turn, he was punished. Whipped. Imprisoned."

I look over at Liam, who seems stung by the words, by the vehemence in them, as he stares at the recent scars on his own arms and hands. It was him, I realize. He was the one who whipped his own brother. Who punished him.

"And we..." continues Sebastian. "We were forbidden to ever speak of him again. He was to be erased from history."

I swallow the lump in my throat. The tension in the room is palpable, and I have so many questions. "How did he betray your Order?"

Sebastian takes a long swig of his drink, then looks at me. "He delved into dark magick and then used his new powers to slay a priest and his disciples. Dozens died by his hand."

I can feel the blood drain from my face. "Why? Why would he do such a thing?"

Liam rubs at the scars on his arm. "The priest was burning women," he says, staring into the fire, the flames growing under his gaze. "He and his followers. If a woman opposed them, angered them in any way, they would declare her a witch and burn her at the stake."

"What the hell? That's...horrifying," I say. "They had to be stopped—"

"Yes, they had to be stopped," Sebastian says firmly, "but not that way. Not through cold-blooded murder. That was not—is not—our way. We could have persuaded the priest to change his ways. Our brother could have—"

"Cole," Derek says, interrupting Sebastian as he stands and faces the group. "His name was Cole. And he did what needed to be done. What we all should have done."

Cole. Cole Night. The man who haunts my dreams has a name. Is this why I feel such a pull to him, because of his connection to this family?

Sebastian frowns. "I recall you having a different opinion at the time, when we found out the truth of his actions." Sebastian's voice is cold. "Cole," he says with derision, "was punished fairly."

"Cole," Liam says softly, caressing the name like something very fragile. "I haven't spoken that name in so very long."

His tender words deflate the argument in the room. Even Sebastian softens, seeing the look on Liam's face, hearing the pain in his voice.

"It may have been Cole that Eve saw," says Elijah. "Or it may have been a look-a-like. A doppelgänger."

"Escaping should have been impossible," Sebastian says.

"And yet, isn't our very existence proof that the impossible is anything but?" Elijah asks, holding out his hands.

"It's not a coincidence that Eve saw him—or someone looking like him—the night of the explosion," Derek says, furrowing his brow in worry. "He could be seeking revenge."

"We mustn't jump to conclusions," Elijah says, "but we can't dismiss the possibility that he escaped." He pauses. "We must be sure. We must go back."

Liam scowls. "I swore I would never return to that forsaken place."

"Then you can stay," Elijah says. "But I will go."

"Go where?" I ask.

"To the birthplace of our Order," Elijah says softly. "To the place our brother was imprisoned."

"You want to travel to England?" asks Liam. "Not exactly an easy trip without a dryad. How do you propose we—"

"I can help," comes a familiar voice. Lily. She's standing in the doorway, leaning on a cane, a blanket draped over her slim shoulders. She looks weak, weary, but her skin is healed of the burns, only some puckered skin remains in the places she was injured the worst.

"Lily!" I stand and walk over to her, hugging her gently.

She chuckles. "I won't break. I'm stronger than I look."

I pull away and study her as the brothers crowd around us. "We've been so worried."

Liam—ever the healer—feels her head and her pulse and studies her carefully.

Lily rolls her eyes. "I'm well, Uncle. I swear," she says, giving Liam's hand a squeeze. "Matilda told me about your arrest, and I overheard what you said about Cole. I can move the castle to England."

"No," says Liam. "You are in no condition to travel."

"But if she can—" Elijah says, ever the pragmatist.

"No," Liam says again, this time more firmly. "I am her healer, and I say she needs at least another week of rest. I will not compromise her health for our convenience."

Even Elijah can't argue with this. No one wants Lily hurt more than she already has been.

The dryad moves into the study to sit on a chair in front of the fire, warming her hands briskly. "Very well," she says. "But I might know someone who can help. Another dryad. Kaya." Lily glances away shyly, her cheeks flushing. "Tell her I sent you, and she should be able to take you where you need to go."

That settles it. It is too late to visit Kaya tonight, but we all agree to touch base with her in the morning and see if she will help us. For now, Elijah gets the details from Lily about where to find the dryad, and Liam makes sure Lily gets back to her tree to rest. Which is what we all need at this point.

Rest. Not a tree to sleep in.

* * *

THE NEXT MORNING, I rise early, grab my cloak and bag, and get ready for our trip. I've always wanted to go to England. I just never imagined I would travel there via dryad magic. But it sure beats international flights.

All four brothers come, as I expected, and so the five of us set out in the carriage. Elijah and Derek sit up front, leaving me in the back with Liam and Sebastian. It's a mostly silent drive as we travel through the town and into a densely populated residential area that lasts for miles before we reach a clearing that leads us to a bumpy dirt road and a lot of forest and hills.

I lean back and close my eyes, replaying all of the new information I've learned over the course of the last few days. My mind keeps returning to Cole. To his face. His eyes. His haunting energy.

When the carriage begins to slow after several hours of butt-bruising travel, I peer out the window and gasp. The Dragon's Breath that fills the sky with color seems to have created a wall of furious green fire that emits such heat we can hardly get closer without burning alive. Already sweat is beading on my forehead and dripping into my eyes. The weirdest thing is that at the base of this green wall of fire, everything just... ends. The trees, the grass, the road. It all disappears. As far as the eye can see.

"It's the edge of The Otherworld," Liam says.

"The edge?" I ask, stunned. "Like... there's nothing beyond that wall?"

He nods.

"Does it encase everything, this wall? Like in a circle or something?"

"There is a perimeter to the world," the fire Druid says. "But most of it is unreachable, at the far edge of steep mountains or great bodies of water. This is the most accessible location."

"Huh. So, it's not a globe, like Earth?" I ask. I've seen maps, of course, in the many books I've read, but I never really considered the shape or magnitude of the world. I never considered that it would have an edge. An end.

"This world is much smaller than yours," Liam says. "And no, it's not a globe."

The idea of this makes my mind spin.

The carriage stops, and we all get out and stretch. My body is bruised, tired, and achy, and I wonder at how people in my world traveled like this throughout history. It's back breaking.

We emerge into a magnificent grove of wood. In a large circle, a fair distance from the fiery edge of the world, smaller saplings sway in the hot wind, and in the middle is a tree much larger than Lily's, its snowy white leaves a sharp contrast to the green hue cast by the Dragon's Breath wall.

There's shouting coming from the center of the grove and as we move towards the conflict we see a dryad, skin green and hair red as blood, yelling at two Enforcers dressed in black cloaks, while a cloven-hooved woman holding a baby cowers behind her.

"These are my clients, and they are getting in," the dryad screams, shielding the woman with her own body. The largest center tree seems to respond to her anger, branches rippling with the dryad's words.

"Kaya," the Enforcer closest to her says, holding out a hand. "The new rules dictate creatures must have a valid permit to enter the Otherworld..."

His voice is familiar, as are the tiny horns on his head. He's the same Enforcer who stopped us to search our carriage the night of the fire.

"This is complete crap," Kaya says. "A dragon egg goes missing and suddenly everyone's a potential criminal. Unless they have enough money to buy their innocence, of course."

The Enforcer looks over to the woman with the baby. "I'm sorry, miss, but you'll have to leave the Otherworld and come back with a permit—"

The woman cries, clutching her child to her chest. "Please, sir. I must stay. We're being hunted. We won't survive if you send us back."

The Enforcer steps forward holding a black wooden rod in one hand. He reaches around the dryad to grab the woman with the other hand. "I'm sure you'll find a way."

"And how is she to get a permit, which can only be issued by your department, if she's not here?" Kaya asks.

The second Enforcer pulls Kaya away from the woman, pinning her to her own tree with his wooden rod, and as he does, it zaps with an electric magnet that shocks Kaya, causing her to scream. "That will be enough argument from the likes of you," he says through gritted teeth, his fist balled, and his body poised for a fight.

The woman in question collapses to her knees, pulling out of the first Enforcer's grasp.

She cries, cradling her screaming infant. "No. Please. I beg you. If I can't stay, take my child..." Her pleas are desperate, grasping at the last remnants of hope for her child, if not herself. She holds the baby out like an offering to a cruel god, and the Enforcer pauses, his face troubled as he glances at his partner who doesn't appear nearly as bothered by conscience. He looks back at the woman but avoids eye contact. "I'm sorry, but I have my own young ones, and if I don't follow the rules, then..."

Enough is enough. I can't watch any more of this.

"Let go of them," I say in my most commanding voice. I walk forward holding up the dragon ring I received earlier. "On order of Ava'Kara, let this woman and her child through."

The Enforcer freezes, his eyes darting between me and the ring I now wield like a weapon.

My heart is pounding in my chest, and I'm soaking my tunic with sweat, the heat of the Dragon's breath rolling off my skin. Behind me I can feel the Night brothers staring, their eyes drilling holes in my back.

While his partner looks annoyed at my intervention, the head Enforcer looks confused as to the right course of action. "But my orders..." he says.

I think he wants a way out of this. I don't believe he wants this woman and her child to die, but he's also a man who follows the law blindly, who values his own safety and health above that of others. He is like so many in my world who refuse to challenge what is clearly wrong, who refuse to look at the whole truth. Willfully blind and just as dangerous, just as cruel and evil as those who actively seek to harm. Maybe even worse, because their evil is subtle, insidious, unintentional. It's caused more by self-interest and an unwillingness to challenge a corrupt system, than by any truly evil aspiration. It is the most prevalent kind of evil, and it enrages me to see it played out with such crass openness. He justifies it to himself because he thinks he's protecting his own family. His own children. But what of this woman? What of her child? What of their lives?

"Your orders are overruled," I say. "The dragons created this quarantine, did they not?"

He nods nervously.

"Then they are in a position to modify it as the need arises. I carry the authority of Ava'Kara. This woman and her child are clearly no threat, and they just as clearly are not hiding any egg. Let them through."

"Yes," he says, glancing once more at my ring. "Let them go."

His partner hesitates, and I see the small sadistic part of him that likes this power. Likes making others feel weaker. Less than. He likes being the big man with the big stick. He doesn't like that I'm taking it away from him.

"Let them go!" The Enforcer repeats again, and his partner pulls away from Kaya and spits on the ground by the tree. Kaya rights herself slowly, her eyes locked on the man who electrocuted her. She looks pissed, and I don't blame her. I'm pissed on her behalf, and I wasn't the one manhandled.

"Welcome to the Otherworld," the head Enforcer says,

tipping his hat to the woman and her child. "I apologize for the—uh—for the misunderstanding."

Misunderstanding. Right. If we hadn't been here, they would have shoved her back into a world where she was being hunted. A world that would have killed them both, likely after doing unspeakable things to her.

He turns to leave, his partner following him. As he walks past me, he mumbles a 'thank you.'

I reach for his arm and pause him. "You might want to find work more suited to you," I whisper, giving him a meaningful look. He nods and continues walking.

The woman stands and comes to me, her eyes streaming with tears. "Thank you. You saved us."

I place a hand on her shoulder. "I hope you find safety here."

She sniffs and nods, and other dryads I didn't see before now come out of their trees to escort care for her and the child.

"Come, love," one says, taking her arm gently. "Let's get you cleaned up and find somewhere for you to stay."

Liam steps up to me, placing a hand on my back, a small smile on his face. "You sure know how to make an entrance."

"I guess you're not the only one with a temper," I say.

Kaya walks over to me and bows her head. "Thank you. It's not often someone bearing one of the dragon's seals actually helps me. Usually they're just trying to shut down my business."

"And what is your business?" I ask, curious.

"Helping folks get to the Otherworld, even if they can't pay their way." She cocks her head. "Especially if they can't pay their way."

"That sounds like a good cause," I say, holding out a hand to shake hers. "I'm Eve Oliver. My friend, Lily, said you may be able to help us."

At Lily's name, Kaya's face lights up. "Lily. How's she doing? Still getting into trouble?"

I pause. Clearly, she hasn't heard. "Lily was...she was injured in the explosion that happened in town. But she's recovering well."

Kaya's face pales. She looks over to the brothers. "You must be her uncles?"

"We are," Derek says, as the rest of them join us.

"She told me about you all," she says.

"Only believe the good things," Derek says, with a grin.

Kaya laughs. "It's all good things. She cares about you a lot."

"It's mutual," Sebastian says. "She's family."

Kaya nods. "Well, Eve Oliver and Lily's Uncles...tell me what you need, and I'll see what I can do. For Lily."

Elijah explains where we need to go.

"A two-way trip, huh?" Kaya strokes her chin, thinking. "Better make it fast. I have somewhere to be."

We follow her to the center tree, the largest of the grove, and we all lay our hands upon it. The bark feels rough against my palms, but I have only a moment to notice it before everything begins to spin and my vision is filled with a blinding light.

We appear under a different sky, dark and filled with thousands of stars. It's a strange sight after being away from the mundane world for so long. I miss the colors of the Dragon's Breath, but it is good to see the stars and a brilliant full moon again. The air is moist and fresh and smells of recently fallen rain against earth and grass.

There's familiarity here, this world that I'm from, but it no longer feels like home, I realize. The Otherworld has become my home. The Night brothers, my family.

"Be quick," says Kaya, leaning against the trunk of her tree and lighting a pipe that she takes a deep inhale from. "Time's a ticking."

I turn to follow the Night brothers, since they seem to know where we are and where we're going. We're surrounded by trees on all sides, deep, shady forests that have come alive with the sounds of the night, of creatures scurrying under brush and birds flitting through the branches.

We walk down a narrow dirt path that leads to old stones peeking from beneath the dirt and moss. The ruins of an ancient building.

"What happened here?" I ask, looking at half-broken columns and empty fountains.

"Time," says Elijah. "It did to this place as it does to all things."

"Not all things," I say. "Not you."

"We, too, are ruins of what we once were." He flexes his hand, and a cool gust of wind picks up. "And yet, for some reason, our powers are returning."

Sebastian nods. "I felt it, too. When I lifted the rocks off Derek."

Elijah glances down at his hands again. "Perhaps Dracula's compulsion was affecting us in more ways than we realized."

Maybe Dracula was limiting their powers, but why? What did he have to gain?

Derek moves to walk by my side, pulling me from my thoughts. "Here is where new apprentices would sleep," he says, pointing to a ruin to the left. More broken columns and shattered walls. "And here used to be the baths. A part of me wishes I could go back in time. Sink my feet into the warm water." He closes his eyes and inhales deeply, and for a moment, he seems somewhere else, a smile on his face.

I notice three statues ahead. Large robed figures, their faces devoid of features, one face broken off. The detail is exquisite. Though they are carved of stone, the fabric on their bodies looks as if it could blow away in the breeze. What artistry and craftsmanship.

When Sebastian sees the statues, he bows his head as if in reverence.

"Who are they?" I ask.

"The three Fates," says Derek. "The Maiden, Mother, and Crone. They were the leaders of our Order."

Elijah nods. "It was said that the Crone could see into the past. The Mother things of the present. And the Maiden things of the future."

I freeze, thinking of Adam and his claims of future sight. "I thought you said no one could see the future," I whisper to Derek.

"No one but the Maiden," he says. "And even then, I have my doubts."

"Where are they now? The Fates?" I ask, my heart thundering in my chest as I try to make sense of what Adam said in relation to this new information. Could there be a connection?

"Gone," says Derek. "Most likely dead. You see, when our brother was imprisoned, it was the beginning of the end. His actions, though deemed a crime, inspired the Maiden to pursue a different course. She became obsessed with stopping the horrible things she would foretell at all costs. Even if it meant doing horrible things in turn."

My thoughts again turn to Adam. To Mary and the baby, dead at his feet. I exchange a worried glance with Derek.

"I am as concerned as you," he says quietly, "regarding recent developments. But I don't know anything more. Only that, once her sisters, the other Fates, learned of what the Maiden was doing, they fought. And no one has seen them since. Without the Fates, the Order collapsed."

"Were you close to them?" I ask.

"To the Fates?" He chuckles. "Not at all. We never even saw their faces. The Fates were...more goddesses than leaders. Something to be grasped at, worshipped even, but never fully understood."

A light rain begins to fall, and it quickly picks up. I look to Derek, but he shrugs. The brewing storm isn't his doing. Nor mine. My cloak is getting soaked and Liam puts an arm around me, his fire powers warming me. "Hurry," he says, guiding me forward, the others following.

He guides us under an archway still intact, towards stairs that lead underground. Before descending, I pause to take a last look at the statues. Three silhouettes in the distance. Rain splashing on their cloaks. Lightning flashing behind them. It reminds me of a dream I once had.

Of a voice in that dream. 'You should have died with your mother.'

Shivering, I descend into darkness.

* * *

WE ENTER a tunnel that smells of mildew and old dirt and something dead. I crinkle my nose and try to acclimate my night vision, but there isn't enough light to do much good. I feel around and find old torches lining the walls, long ago made useless by time, the elements, and lack of use. But with a flick of his hand, Liam lights them all.

"You'll have to teach me how to do that," I say.

Liam nods with a smile.

As each fire comes to life, the hall lights up, revealing crumbling old stone and the remains of dead rats.

I grab one of the torches since I don't have the see-in-the-dark superpowers they do, and we travel deeper and deeper. I do my best to avoid stepping on anything dead... or alive, as we walk.

"What will you do if...if your brother is still here?" I ask, my voice echoing off the walls.

Liam glances at me, his brow furrowed. Sebastian avoids my gaze and Elijah and Derek keep walking.

"Will you free him?" I ask, pressing the issue. "If he's still imprisoned?"

"Never," says Sebastian, without looking at me. "He would be a danger to us. To you."

"We would have to vote," says Elijah, glancing at his brother with a frown.

"Over a thousand years of imprisonment," says Liam. "I think Cole has paid enough."

I look to Derek, who answers after a moment. "Perhaps Cole deserves to be free," he says. And then more softly, "Perhaps we should be the ones to pay."

I study his solemn face, his wounded eyes, and I reach for his hand and squeeze it. Despite our recent arguments, he squeezes back. It was only a few days ago that these men were ready to take their own lives in payment for their sins. Their demons still haunt them...even if they've chosen to fight on.

"We're here," says Liam, and I follow him through an opening and into an antechamber. It's a massive stone room with painted carvings in the walls, most of which have faded with time.

But there's one I can still make out.

A woman's face framed by flowing silver hair that match her eyes.

I catch Elijah staring at it, then he quickly glances away.

In the center of the room a black, steel sarcophagus hangs from the ceiling, wrapped in silver chains.

I shiver at the sight of it, and the brothers all stop, staring at it as well.

I can't even imagine what it would do to a person to be locked in that for over a thousand years. I would go mad. Anyone would.

Even the shadows seem to swirl around it as if they, too, fear getting close to the monstrous prison. There's a dark energy in this room. A dangerous poison that creeps over my skin and bleeds into me.

"The bindings have been tampered with," Elijah says, taking a step closer. "It's closed but..." He reaches out, touching the black steel. The chains around the sarcophagus drop and he pulls it open.

It's empty.

My heart leaps into my throat when someone behind us begins clapping. I spin around, and there I see him.

The man from my dreams.

Pale skin in the torchlight. Dark tattoos covering his arms. A black cloak wrapped around him.

And eyes like the night.

Eyes that can steal your soul.

Cole.

THE BEGGAR QUEEN

A star's light shines the brightest, When it's starting to collapse.
~Supernova by Erin Hanson

SEBASTIAN STEPS FORWARD FIRST, his fists clenched, muscles tense. I can feel the ground beneath us tremble with his anger. "Are you here to take your revenge?" he asks.

Cole smirks, looking unconcerned. "No, *mon frère*. I'm here to help."

His French accent surprises me. I was expecting him to sound more British like his brothers.

"Really?" Sebastian doesn't sound convinced. The tension in the room is so thick I'm gagging on it. "Then why not reveal yourself sooner? Why all these cat and mouse games? We know you were at the festival."

Cole shrugs, leaning against the wall casually. Is he really this calm, I wonder? Or just good at faking it?

"I thought this would be the more appropriate location

for our reunion," he says. "A walk through memory lane, as it were."

Something in another part of the ruins crashes down as Sebastian struggles to control his powers. "This is just a game to you, isn't it? You enjoy toying with people, you always have. Tell me, how did you escape?"

Cole glances at the sarcophagus, and for the first time I see an emotion other than arrogance ripple across his face. Fear. But it's gone in an instant. "A thousand years is a long time. Perhaps the binding wore off..."

"Liar—"

Derek places a hand on Sebastian's arm, giving him a warning glance. "Control yourself, brother," he says softly. "Or you'll bring the whole place down on our heads."

Sebastian takes a deep breath and steps back, deliberately unclenching his fists.

Derek studies Cole, his expression a mixture of wariness and hope. "Why help us?" he asks, in a much less combative tone than Sebastian.

Cole steps forward, holding the palms of his hands open in petition. "Because I didn't do it, even though you seem to think I did. This heist was masterful...but not my own. And I would never take credit for someone else's work. You should know that about me, *mon frère*."

"That's a very generous attitude, all things considered," Derek says. "What do you want from us, in return for this help?"

"I want what I have always wanted. Peace between us, brothers. My family back." His voice cracks, and either he is a skilled performer, or he's being sincere.

"After what you did?" Sebastian spits, his words creating another shift of stone and rock around us.

Cole scoffs. "After what I did? I stopped a murdering stain on the fabric of humanity. What about what you did to me?" Cole asks, coming face to face with Sebastian. "You betrayed your own brother. Your flesh and blood? And for what?"

Even Sebastian is put in his place by Cole's words, and he looks away, unable to face him.

Liam stares at the scars on his arms, and Elijah and Derek look thoughtful. Lost in past memories.

In the silence, a flash hits me, making my head spin and my stomach clench. As I take a step closer to Cole, the effects ease, and I realize something with certainty. Something the Night brothers aren't going to like. "We need him," I say, through clenched teeth. The closer I get to Cole, the better I feel, until I am standing inches from him, our gazes locked. "We need him to solve this and save Liam."

Cole studies me, his lips curling into a smile. "Smart woman. *Et belle.* My brothers showed unexpected wisdom in bringing you into the family."

Though we're not making physical contact, I feel his touch nonetheless, as if his hands are caressing my face. I blink and take a step back, my senses rattled by this intense intimacy I'm experiencing against all logic.

"He could be useful," Elijah says. "Whether he is indeed guilty, or as innocent as he claims, he could help in gaining access to our other suspects."

Cole doesn't break eye contact with me as he responds. "What are your leads?"

"None of your business," Sebastian says, glaring at Elijah. "We shouldn't be sharing anything with him. We don't know what he's up to and we can't trust him."

Elijah shrugs. "What can we lose by seeing what he has to offer? We haven't got many options and even less time in which to solve this."

"Elijah's right," Derek says. "We must explore all possibilities, and if Cole can help, so be it."

Liam steps forward, his eyes haunted. "If Eve says we need him, I trust her."

Sebastian throws up his hands in defeat and crosses his arms over his chest, sulking as Elijah answers Cole. "The Collector could be behind this, and if he isn't, there's a good chance he knows something."

Cole nods. "And?"

"And the Beggar Queen," Derek says. "She's been at odds with the dragons for as long as anyone can remember. She had the motive and the means to pull this off."

Cole finally breaks eye contact with me to look at his brothers, and in that instant, I feel his touch—his presence —vanish from my body. I release a breath I didn't realize I was holding and shiver. Liam puts a protective arm around my shoulder, his heat and strength a comfort.

Cole paces, his finger on his chin. "The Collector will be tricky. He is hard to get close to, even for me, and keeps his secrets well hidden. But you know I can get you in to see the Beggar Queen, as you call her, though she would never refer to herself as such."

"What is she the queen of?" I ask.

"The lost and forgotten," Cole says softly.

"Indeed," Elijah says, though he doesn't sound particularly happy about it. He turns to the rest of us. "I think we may need him."

"I don't," Sebastian says, stepping forward once again. "He betrayed us once before and he will again."

I pull away from Liam to stand before Sebastian, placing a hand on his chest. "It's Liam's future on the line. He should decide."

Everyone looks to the fire Druid, who sighs and turns to Cole.

I already know what Liam will decide. Not just because he wants to get out of this mess, but because he wants to atone for his own sins.

"We have no way of knowing your true motives," he tells Cole. "Even still, I say we give you a chance."

Cole smiles a wolfish grin.

"The Order would never have accepted this," Sebastian roars, causing the sarcophagus to crash to the ground, startling everyone.

Derek frowns. "Look around, brother. We are all that's left. The Order is gone."

And with that, the decision is made. We make haste back to the Otherworld with Cole in tow. Kaya seems impatient to get on with her other errands, though she catches my eye as we head to the carriage and nods briefly at me, mouthing a simple 'thank you.' The woman and child we helped earlier are both being cared for by the dryads, the child nursing peacefully as the mother rests against one of the trees, and I hope that they find a good life here. That their terror and pain will be things of the past as they try to rebuild.

We are all shaped and haunted by our pasts. I haven't yet lived thirty years, and already I feel the weight of my life tugging at my heart, clouding my mind, shaping my choices for good or ill. I can't imagine having hundreds of years piling on me, like dirt on a coffin, burying me in the darkness of my past decisions, stealing away my breath with each handful of years dropped on me.

What must each of the Night brothers be feeling as we climb into the carriage and set off to meet the Beggar Queen? What memories must be resurfacing as they all face their own darkness?

Cole sits in the front with Elijah, guiding the carriage to our destination, since he's the only one who knows where we're going. Sebastian, Liam, and Derek sit in the back with me, though all are quiet and lost in thought.

I don't want to disturb them, but I reach for Sebastian's hand, who sits beside me, and he takes it, though he doesn't look my way. But with the touch, his shoulders seem to relax just a fraction, and I hope that he can find some peace in all this mess.

They have their brother back, and it's a mixed bag for them. I get it. All too well. I kind of have my twin back, but I still don't know how to feel about all he's done...all he's become. Is evil done in the name of justice justifiable? Do we have the right to take a life preemptively to protect future innocents? Do we have the right to take a life in righteous justice when it goes against the laws of the land? At what point do we need to stop blindly following other people's rules for what's expected of us and take a stand for what we believe is right?

Both Cole and Adam clearly believe their actions—their murders—were justified. Righteous, even. And yet I am left with questions my soul cannot answer. Questions all my reading and all my knowledge and all my intelligence cannot find a definitive solution for.

Maybe there is no answer. Maybe the whole point is to

question, and to keep questioning as we strive to find our way in this messy world.

After spending too much time studying the brothers and thinking about Cole, I turn my attention to the window and watch as the landscape changes. Where before we crossed through either wide expanses of open land or crowded but comfortably situated populated areas, now we move into the type of area I haven't seen in this world before, though I'm familiar enough with it from my own. Ruined buildings scatter the landscape, climbing with ivy and covered in moss as nature takes back its own. The roads are dirt and full of holes and rocks, making the journey dangerous and painful. As we come closer to the town, the poverty and unsuitable living conditions become more glaring. Malnourished children of various races run around naked, covered in dirt and slime. Entire families live in shelters constructed with bits of stick propping up palm branches as makeshift roofs. Insects buzz everywhere, more well fed than any of the people living here. What little clothing exists consists of torn rags hanging off emaciated bodies.

Though there's plenty of wilderness, there's little in the way of farmland or food sources. It's clear no Enforcer has been here in ages, if ever. Nothing has been done to create suitable living arrangements for the people here. The world has forgotten them.

We reach the end of the road and have to disembark and make our way on foot from there. The smell hits me first. Rot and bodily waste mix with the smell of cooking grains and unwashed children. I stifle the urge to gag and take shallow breaths. Cole steps up next to me, leading the way down a small alley.

"This is what coloring within the lines gets you, *mon cher*," he says. His eyes are full of pain as he looks around at those suffering. "Playing by the rules, following those in command...it only serves those in power. These are the people who pay the price."

We reach the end of the alley where two basilisks guard one of the only standing structures in this village. They're both dressed in dirty white robes, their large serpentine bodies framing a double door made of ashen wood. They are more snake than human, and like the guard who died at the nest, they wear blindfolds over their eyes. Their reptilian tongues flick out of their mouths, tasting the air.

"It hassss been sssssome time, Cole," one says, his words coming out as a hiss.

"It's good to see you, Raz. How are the kids?"

Raz nods his head. "Sssstrong, like their mother. And you? What do you sssssseek?"

"We request an audience with Lyx, if she is able to see us," Cole says with respect in his voice.

The second basilisk hisses and turns her face to the other Night brothers. "I know you," she says. "Traitorsssss to our causssse. You are not welcome here." Then she turns to me, testing the air with her tongue. "You, I do not know."

"Bron," Cole says to the female, "this is Eve Oliver. She's with me."

"Eve Oliver," Bron says, testing my name aloud.

The basilisks pause, and the two of them touch their heads together, whispering through hisses.

Raz raises his head to speak. "Cole and the woman may enter. The resssst musssst remain."

Sebastian steps forward and I cringe, knowing this is not going to go well.

"I'm not leaving her alone with Cole. He's dangerous," Sebastian says.

"It's my life on the line," Liam says. "I should be the one to go."

"Guys, I'll be okay. No good will come from making a scene. This is our one chance to talk to her. Trust me, okay? I can take care of myself," I say, giving both of them a reassuring hand squeeze.

Then Cole, not helping matters in the least, throws an arm over my shoulder. "And I'll be sure to look out for her, too. She'll be well cared for in my very capable hands."

The earth tremors slightly as Sebastian clenches his jaw and fists, ready to strike out at his brother.

I slip away from Cole and glare at him, then shoot a look at Sebastian. "Wait for us at the carriage," I say.

He nods, then turns sharply away. Derek and Elijah give me half-hearted smiles but say nothing.

Liam grabs my arm. "Be careful. With all of them."

I nod, then follow Cole, leaving the others behind.

We enter through the double doors into a large room. Intricate rugs are intermittently spread over the dirt-packed floors and pewter lamps with colored glass hang on the walls. The air is perfumed with burning herbs and scented oils, and at the end of the room several people are lounging on purple and red pillows. In the center of the group is the Beggar Queen—Lyx. Though she, too, sits on a pillow, a goblet of wine at her side, she stands out amongst them all. Her gown is pure white. Her hair is long and silver—the same color as her eyes. She glows like a star against the night sky. Like a diamond.

"I recognize her," I whisper to Cole. "Her likeness was carved into the ruins in England."

He nods as we approach.

The queen stands and opens her arms to greet us. Cole walks into them, giving the woman an affectionate hug. She pats his face, studying him, then tilts her head and kisses his forehead. "Watch yourself, my son. You are teetering close to the abyss."

"That's the only way to truly find balance," Cole says, with a charming grin.

She laughs, and he steps aside, so I can approach.

"I have heard rumors of you," the queen says, bringing me in for an unexpected embrace.

When she releases me, I step back and clear my throat. "Good ones, I hope?"

She smirks. "Strange ones. Regarding your abilities." She raises an eyebrow, as if in question. But I have no answers for her.

"Were you a Druid?" I ask, changing the subject.

She nods. "Long ago. But I renounced that Order...much like Cole, here."

I glance at Cole, then back at her. I know why he left the Order, but... "Why did you leave?"

She sits and invites us to join her, then pours us each a cup of wine. Once we are settled, she answers, "The Order claimed to help the people, but more and more, I saw that help go mostly to the wealthy and privileged. I left to help those who needed it the most."

I take a sip of the wine, realizing how thirsty I am after

all the dusty travel. "I take it you and the other Night brothers didn't part on good terms?"

"No," she says. "We did not."

Of course. This is why she won't see them. "I don't know what happened between you all...but Liam is being accused of a crime he didn't commit, and I intend to prove his innocence."

The queen takes a sip of wine. "Are you a lawyer, as well?"

"I work for the firm," I say. "And I was hoping you could help me. I'm looking for information about the stolen dragon egg."

She cocks her head, studying me. "And what makes you think I know anything?"

Well, shit. I can't come right out and say she's a suspect, but I have the sense that anything less than the truth won't sit well with her, either. "To be honest, we're short on leads and even shorter on time. You're someone with influence and authority. Someone who inspires those who don't fit into the system. Whoever took the egg likely wanted to throw a wrench into the power structure of this world. That seems like something you might know about."

"Very well put," she says with a smile. "You have clearly learned the art of speaking to the heart of a truth."

"So, will you help?" I ask again. "Liam doesn't deserve to be punished for this."

"Who is to weigh the scales on what someone does or does not deserve?" she asks. "How heavy is Liam's soul? How would it compare to the weight of this punishment, I wonder?"

"Do you believe you can know that?" I ask frankly. "Do

you have the measure of every person in your presence? Let alone the measure of one you haven't seen in such a long time? You formed your opinion of Liam and the other brothers a thousand years ago. And maybe at the time it was valid. But do you not believe people can change? That they can redeem themselves? When was the last time you reconsidered your own misjudgments?"

Cole is staring at me. I can feel his dark gaze like a physical touch. But I don't turn to look at him. Instead, I stare into the silver eyes of the woman before me, unwaveringly.

Finally, she sighs, and leans back, breaking contact. "I don't know who has the egg," she says. But there are words left unspoken, as if she is not telling me all she knows.

"Please," I say. "If you know anything more, share it. They're locking down the Otherworld. Until the egg is found, people who seek refuge will be denied. As bad as is it for refugees here, imagine what they face in the mundane world. They are feared, hunted, killed. They need your help. If not for Liam or me, then for them."

"Oh child, you have no idea, do you? You really don't know."

I straighten my back, staring at the queen. "Don't know what?"

"The dragons," she says softly. "The dragons always want more power. Especially Dath'Racul. He seeks to increase taxes. Reduce support to the poor. For a while, his efforts were considered too extreme. But no longer. Not with the egg missing. Now the people embrace his ways. As does the Council."

"You think...Dath'Racul stole the egg himself?" I ask. "To tighten government control?"

She shrugs. "Possibly. Or maybe one of the other dragons. Water. Earth. Fire. Air. Darkness. They used to want to help the world. But at some point, they decided to help themselves first."

She lowers her voice. "I asked my brothers and sisters to change their ways, I begged them. But they would not. So, I am here...with those they have forgotten...and they are in their palaces of crystal and gold."

Her brothers and sisters? I look at the queen of beggars again, seeing her as if for the first time as a vision overtakes me and reveals to me the queen's true self.

In the darkness of my mind a brilliant silver-white dragon stands before me, radiant like a star, vast as a mountain. She glows with light that emanates from within, casting out the shadows with her very presence.

"The dragon of light..." I say in awe.

She nods, smiling gently. "I was. Yes. But even I was not bright enough to burn the darkness out of the Order, or out of the Council of Dragons. I am sorry I cannot help you further, but I wish you the best in your quest, daughter." She leans in to kiss my cheek, and I feel a spark between us. Her eyes widen in wonder and surprise, and she studies me carefully as we are escorted out the room and back into the alley.

"She was our mentor," Cole tells me as we walk back to the carriage where the others have gone to wait. "For a while, anyway. She taught Druids about the light. My brothers had a propensity for the other elements. Fire. Water. Earth. Air. But I..." He holds up a hand and a ball of white light appears, lighting up the dark alley.

"You were a light Druid," I say, realization dawning on me.

"Once," he says, his voice soft. Reflective. "Very long ago." He drops his hand, and the light fades, drawing us into darkness once more.

THE FLAME

She, In the dark, Found light Brighter than many ever see.
  ~Helen Keller by Langston Hughes

AFTER SOME DELIBERATION, it's decided Cole will come back to the castle with us.

I fill them all in on what Lyx said, and now we need to decide what to do next.

"Investigating the dragons will be tricky, at best," Derek says, as we bump along the road.

I rub my backside, confident there will be bruises. "Any chance we can get some, I don't know, cushions back here? I'm going to be black and blue after today."

"If you need a massage, I have excellent hands," Cole says, holding said hands up with a wink.

He's not wrong. They are fine looking hands. Strong with long fingers. A musician's hands.

Elijah and Derek both frown.

"We can make it more comfortable," Elijah says. "I've

actually been considering some upgrades to the carriage. Just haven't had time."

"Thanks," I say. "If you need help, let me know. I'm pretty handy."

Elijah raises an eyebrow. "I wouldn't have guessed."

"I'm not just a pretty face and a smart brain," I say. "I have other skills."

Cole throws an arm around my shoulders. "That doesn't surprise me at all. In fact, I look forward to learning all about your other skills."

His attention is flattering and disconcerting and I'm just glad the two hotheads up front aren't here to witness it. Though with their vampire hearing, Liam and Sebastian probably aren't missing much.

Derek clears his throat. "Back to the dragons?"

"Yes, this will need to be handled very carefully," Elijah says. "They are too powerful to come at directly. We need to be discreet in our questions, and we can't let anyone suspect that we are going after them."

"Or what?" I ask. "Shouldn't the people have the right to question their leadership?"

Cole smirks. "Not here. This isn't a democracy. This is an autocracy. It may seem the Dragon Council is balanced, but really Dath'Racul runs things, and keeps the other dragons under his thumb. Lyx'Ara dissented by trying to put their focus back on the people rather than their own personal power and look how that turned out for her. The Dragon of Darkness mostly holes up in his dungeon and doesn't much care for the rest of the world. And the others are too cowed by Dath to stop him in his pursuits. Especially now."

"So, they can do anything to anyone and there's no one to hold them accountable?" I ask.

"Pretty much," Cole says.

"That's not entirely true," says Elijah, pointedly. "We do have some checks and balances. We have a legal system set up with rules. There is a way to work within the system to change things."

Cole scoffs. "Right. How's that going for you? Or did you give up helping people when you became vampires?"

"We are defense attorneys," Derek reminds him. "It's our job to help people who are in trouble."

Cole leans back, crossing his arms over his chest. "That's an interesting choice of career for men who were more than willing to throw their own brother under the bus. Where was my defense when I needed one the most?"

No one has an answer for him, and so we travel in silence the rest of the way home.

The tension is thick when we arrive and head inside the castle. Matilda is waiting by the door, her eyes red and swollen like she's been crying.

When she sees Cole, she cries out, holding her arms open. "My boy. You've come home at last."

I don't entirely know what I was expecting, but when Cole embraces her and his eyes well up with tears, I'm shocked. I had no idea they were so close. There's so much to their history I don't know. So much I will likely never know.

"*Grand-mère*," he says with raw emotion. "I'm sorry I didn't come sooner."

He pulls away and she pats him on his cheek like a child. "You look good. I know you've been through more than most, but you've always been strong. Brave. I knew you'd come out of it okay."

Cole looks away frowning. "Well, I came out of it at least."

Matilda leads him in by the hand. "I hope your tastes haven't changed too much. I've prepared all your favorite foods."

We follow them into the dining room, and my stomach rumbles loud enough to draw looks from everyone.

Cole pulls out a seat next to his. "Join me? Have my brothers not been keeping you fed? Their appetites have changed, but you cannot live on blood."

Sebastian bristles at that. "She has plenty of food to eat anytime she wants."

Cole rolls his eyes and we both sit. The others all do as well, and Matilda brings out food for those of us who eat and blood for those who don't.

Lily makes a surprise visit, joining us. She smiles shyly at Cole and holds out a hand. "We haven't met. I'm Lily. The Nights adopted me into their family, years ago."

Cole stands and kisses her hand gallantly. "*Enchantè*. It is a pleasure to make your acquaintance. I've always found dryads very magical."

She nods then takes a seat across from us.

"May I ask, how is it you have a French accent, while your brothers don't?"

There's an uncomfortable silence as they glance at each other, and it's Matilda who answers for them.

"Cole spent most of his childhood training in France," she says. "He was particularly gifted with his magick at an early age and was sent to apprentice there."

"I fell in love with the country," Cole says. "If not with my master."

Matilda frowns. "I'm sorry, my boy. If we had known…"

Cole shrugs. "It is in the past, is it not? This is the time for new beginnings."

As we begin eating, a cry interrupts us from the other room. Liam jumps up, setting his goblet of blood down. "Excuse me."

Cole looks over, confused. "There's a baby here?"

"I'm surprised you didn't already know," Sebastian says bitterly. "You seem to know everything else despite having been gone for a thousand years."

Cole sips at his wine and smiles. "I've done due diligence, but some rumors clearly haven't reached me yet." He looks to me. "Is the child yours?"

I blush and shake my head. "Liam's. She is half human, though."

Liam returns with the baby bundled in his arms. His expression softens as he looks at his daughter. "She just needed a change and a bottle," he says, feeding her as he takes his seat.

Cole can't take his eyes off of them. "I'm an…uncle?"

The four other brothers look at him, but only Liam nods. "It would appear so."

We eat in silence, and when Matilda brings us apple pie fresh from the oven, Cole moves to sit next to Liam. "May I…would it be okay if I held her?"

The two lock eyes, and I can see the war in Liam. The desire to protect his child. His suspicion of Cole. But also…his own guilt. His desire to reconcile with his brother. Finally, he nods and hands the child over. "Make sure to support her head, and here, curve your arm so she can lay in it."

Liam adjusts Cole's arm and arranges Alina in his arms. Cole sits next to Liam, studying his niece, cooing to her and letting her play with his finger.

"She's strong," he says, smiling. "A mighty grip."

She gurgles and then quite suddenly a tiny burst of flames shoot from her hands, singeing the edges of Cole's hair. He handles it in stride, laughing as he uses his free hand to pat at his head. We are all staring, wide-eyed.

Cole looks around. "I take it this is new?"

Liam nods. "She's never shown powers before."

Matilda shakes her head. "We're going to need to fire-proof her room. Goodness knows what she'll be up to now."

Liam's grinning like a fool. "She's a fire element. I wasn't sure if she'd have active powers, being half human."

"She takes after her father," I say with a smile, and Liam smiles back, his happiness so pure it swells my heart.

"Speaking of powers," I say. "I've become something of the Otherworld freak. Everyone we meet wants to know what I am. What I can do. I don't know what to say, and I feel like my powers are just out of control. I need help learning how to use them. How to control them. How to even figure out what they are. Will you all help me?"

Matilda nods, finishing the last bite of her pie. "I was going to suggest this myself. It seems, my dear, that you have power from many of the elements. Maybe all of them. This is incredibly rare. It makes you a magical anomaly of sorts. I think it best you train with each of my grandsons to learn to control the different elements and understand your limits."

My body buzzes with a new excitement. I will finally learn what I can do. Maybe this will even help me understand what I am. Who I am. And just maybe it will also help me understand my brother better.

Deep down, in a place I don't like to look at much, I also fear what I will become if I unleash my powers.

Will I become like my twin? Willing to do anything— no matter how atrocious—if I believe it will serve the greater good? But how can anyone be assured of that? How can anyone truly, in their soul, justify evil deeds for the sake of what might be?

"I can train with you a bit tonight," Liam says, pulling my attention back to the conversation.

Derek nods. "That's a good idea. I need Elijah to help with some research. We have to start preparing for the trial."

"I can take care of the baby while you two are training," Sebastian says. "I haven't had much time with my niece."

Matilda rises. "Well now, that's been settled. Cole, your room is readied for you. Come with me, and then you and I can have a nice cup of tea and catch up."

Cole hands the baby over to Sebastian and follows Matilda out, sparing one last glance at me, his expression slightly haunted.

Derek and Elijah leave for the study, and Liam takes my hand as we head to the forge. "It's best to practice fire magic in a place suited for heat and fire. We wouldn't want to burn anything down."

I can't imagine my powers being strong enough to do that kind of damage, but it's a smart precaution.

The forge is a large building adjacent to the castle and smells of hot metal and burning wood. No one is here, but there is work being done. The fire is stoked, metal is being melted, cooled, and hammered into different shapes. I stand, gaping. "Ghosts?" I ask.

Liam nods. "They use the forge to make things useful to the castle. Every once in awhile, we'll find a new sword or knife, meticulously made in the finest craftsmanship. We believe one of the ghosts must have been a master metal worker in their time."

"That's... incredible." I swipe my forehead with the sleeve of my shirt, mopping the sweat off my brow, and I wonder if improving my fire element will help me handle heat better.

Liam seems completely fine. Not a drop of sweat on him.

"How do you do that?" I ask.

"Do what? We haven't even started yet."

"Not sweat," I say. "I feel like I'm in a sauna."

He laughs, and, god, I love the sound of it. He should laugh more often.

"I don't know. I guess it's an inherent part of my powers."

"I hope it's contagious," I say, swiping again at my forehead as sweat burns my eyes.

"Let's see what you can do," he says, standing in front of me. "Remember, I'm fireproof, so don't worry about losing control. I've got you."

That does make me feel better. "How do I start?"

"Imagine a flame in the center of your body, deep within. Tap into that flame, letting it flare within you until you can feel it in your hands," he says.

I close my eyes and attempt to do what he says, but instead of fire, a strong wind blows around us.

I sigh and open my eyes. "Wrong element."

He chuckles. "But close. Fire and air are aligned. Air helps stoke fire's flames. Fire can't breathe without air. Keep trying."

This time he stands behind me and wraps his arms around me, holding my hands in his. I close my eyes and lean into him as his body heats up. I feel his flames, simmering in his palms, glancing against my flesh, but it doesn't burn me. It warms me.

His lips are against my ear, his voice soft as he guides me. "Do you feel the fire in me?" he asks.

I nod.

"It's in you as well. You just have to find it. Unlike us, you have more than one element at work, so it might be confusing. But it's there. Let my flame light your way."

His heat burns through my own resistance and I slide deeper into myself. There, in the center of my soul, I see the elemental powers that animate my magic. My breathing hitches as I realize it's not just a few of the elements I can access.

It's all of them.

All six.

I embrace the fire and feel the balancing tonic of earth and air. The light in me is strong and powerful. But it is the darkness, lurking beneath, floating like a black cloud, that scares me. I shy away from it, unwilling to touch it lest it corrupt me and turn me into something I do not want to be. I focus back on the fire, urging the tiny flame to grow.

After a moment, I feel Liam's arms tighten around me.

"Open your eyes," he whispers.

I do, slowly, and at first all I see is his fire dancing on his palms. Then I look more closely and realize my hand also hold the flame.

"I'm doing it," I say, excitement surging with me.

"You are," he says, smiling against my cheek. "Now see if you can control it. Try to throw the flame at the wall."

"What if I break something?" I ask.

"Trust me, this place has seen it all. It's indestructible. At least, by fire."

I nod and focus my mind on the ball of fire in my hand. With a flick of my wrist, I toss it, and to my surprise, I'm successful! The flaming ball flies across the room, slams into the stone wall, and fizzles out at impact.

Liam steps back and grins, his flames gone now. "You're a fast study," he says. "That took an incredible amount of control."

"That was amazing," I say, studying my hands like they might reveal all the answers. "I've never felt like that before. When I used my powers before, it was by accident. I didn't know what I was doing. I still don't know how I did what I did. But now, I could feel the control, the power. It's raw and rusty, but still…I did it."

He nods. "You'll get more proficient at it with time. Now you need to practice."

And so we do. For the next hour, Liam has me throwing balls of fire, setting things on fire, dancing flames off my fingertips, and finally, he instructs me to light a candle. This proves to be the hardest of all. I melt a few candles down to the wick in my attempts to light them.

"I can't do this," I say. "I feel like I could burn a small

village down, but I can't seem to light one stupid candle."

"You're tired, and smaller things require more control. You can't just unleash it all at once, you have to learn to manage your power. You'll get there. Let's pause for tonight. You look like you could use a bath and a rest."

A bath sounds amazing, and Liam walks me up to my room, gently kisses me goodnight, and leaves me to tend to myself.

As predicted, I am bruising. Badly. I bathe, letting the hot water wash away some of my pain. Moon perches on the bath next to me, meowing to be pet as I relax, and I give him some love. Then I get out and put a bathrobe on. But I'm not ready to sleep, though I should.

Instead, I make my way to Liam's room, where I hear him playing the violin. The music seeps into my soul and brings up a flood of emotion. I wait by the door, letting the last melancholic notes fade before I knock.

He's only wearing pants when he opens it, and his eyes widen in surprise at seeing me.

Suddenly I feel self-conscious. "I was hoping—as a healer—you might have something for my bruises?"

He nods, letting me in. "Show me," he says.

I suck in my breath, and then I undo my robe and let it drop to my feet, so that I'm standing before him naked. His eyes widen, and he stares at me for a long moment. "You're...you're so beautiful, Eve." His breath hitches on my name and I feel a new kind of fire alight within me.

I turn to show him my back and it's his turn to suck in a breath. "I will make sure Elijah does something to fix the carriage before you have to ride in it again," he says, frowning. "If you lay on the bed, I'll apply a cream to the bruises that should help you heal faster."

It's cool out, with a gentle breeze coming in through the open window, but all I feel is the heat igniting within me as I lay face down on his bed and breathe in his scent. I hear him moving around the room, and then feel as he sits on the bed, his body pressing against mine.

"Is it okay if I touch you?" he asks.

Right now, I want him to do a lot more than just touch me, but everything feels as if it's teetering on the edge of something important, and so I whisper 'yes' and wait.

He's been all about consent since I chewed him out for biting me against my will.

Now I crave the feel of his teeth sliding into my flesh.

But I settle for his warm hands as he slowly rubs something minty smelling into my back. Instantly, the aches and pains begin to fade. He's skilled with his hands, massaging my muscles with expert technique, easing out the stiffness and knots that I carry with me almost always. He runs his fingers between my ribs, from my spine to the sides of my breasts. As he works his way lower, every nerve in my body comes alive. His palms caress the dip in my back and then his hands cup my ass, rubbing and massaging until the pain is completely gone, and all I feel is a desperate arousal at his closeness, his touch, the vulnerability of being naked here with him.

It's quiet as he continues down my legs, fingers grazing between my thighs, coming so close to where I really want them to be, but then pulling back. He completes the massage at my feet, then lightly runs his hands over my body once more, letting out a spark of his magic and sending flashes of warmth over me.

"How do you feel?" he asks, his throat thick with his own desire.

I turn over and lay naked, facing him. "Amazing. I hope you're going to do my front as well?"

His pupils dilate and the bulge in his pants grows. This time he begins at my feet and slowly works his way up my legs. His gaze is locked on mine as he moves over me, straddling my legs so he can be in a better position. When he reaches my hips, he pauses. "How deep of a massage do you want?" he asks, his voice nearly breathless.

"As deep as you can give," I say.

He moans softly at my words, and his hands slide between my legs. He repositions himself so that I'm spread before him, and he teases at the flesh there, grazing but not penetrating.

Dipping his head closer to me, he takes a nipple into his mouth, and the sudden wave of pleasure that hits me makes my hips arch.

He moves his lips up to my neck, raking my skin with his now-elongated teeth.

I wrap my arms around him, pulling him closer to me. "I want you," I say.

He raises his head to look at me. "I have wanted you since I tasted you," he says.

He pulls away long enough to take his pants off, and I study his beautiful—and fully aroused—body. It's a masterpiece of perfection. One that could have been sculpted from marble. I run my hand over his chest and abs as he positions himself above me. Then his hand dips between my legs, and he kisses me deeply while using his fingers to pleasure me.

As the tension mounts, just before release, he removes his hand and pushes his hips into me as he sinks his teeth into my neck.

I cry out, my body pressing against his, my fingers digging into his back, as I am gripped by the best orgasm of my life. The heat between us is so intense it's nearly smoldering.

After a few minutes, he pulls me up, onto his lap, and we face each other as we continue making love. His hands explore my body, and I am consumed by him in every way.

Another orgasm grips me, and as I give into it, so, too, does he. We ride that wave together until we are both spent.

It's only then that I realize I smell something burning, and we both look at the bed and realize it's ablaze.

Instantly, I channel the water element within me, in the same way I controlled the fire, and I summon enough to drown the flames, though I also succeed in soaking most of the bed.

"This is the first time I've set my bed on fire," he says, holding me in his arms, my head on his chest.

"Or I set it on fire," I say.

"I have a feeling it was both of us." He kisses my forehead, sighing deeply. "I've never met anyone like you, Eve. No one has ever made me feel this way before."

"Not even Mary?" I ask. I instantly regret bringing up her name, and all the joy I felt a moment before crashes into regret as I consider the awful secret I'm keeping from him. My stomach twists as I fight with myself over what I should do about Adam and Liam.

"Not even Mary," he says. "I've had other lovers. I've lived a long life. But I've never had this." He tilts my head up so I'm looking into his eyes. "I've never had you."

THE BALL

How much can come And much can go, And yet abide the world! ~Emily Dickinson

"She has a right to make her own decisions!" Cole's voice carries through the halls and I pause outside the library door, my flash tingling through my body.

They're talking about me.

"It's not worth the risk," Liam shouts back, and I can picture the two of them—Liam and Cole—staring each other down. Liam with his fiery temper and ginger good looks, Cole with his almost eerie calmness and dark, mysterious sexiness. Cole will keep his voice level, his emotions in check, which will just further infuriate Liam.

"The egg could be there," Cole says, his voice firm but level. "And she's the only one who got an invite. Of course, she should go. If she's willing. Either way, it should be her choice, not yours."

"Liam's right," Sebastian says, undoubtedly folding his

arms over his muscular chest. "She'd be surrounded by the powerful but shady elite of our society. It's dangerous."

Cole snickers. "I think she's proven she can take care of herself. You underestimate her. You all do."

I sigh and push the door open. "What's too dangerous for me?" I ask the five Night brothers, who all pause their argument to stare at me.

"Well? Anyone want to explain?"

Cole smiles, turning the full weight of his natural seductiveness towards me and causing my knees to turn to jelly. He grabs something from Liam's hand and walks over, his gaze locked on mine. "You have been invited to a ball, mon cher," he says with a flourish, holding out a golden ticket.

I take it from him and study it.

At first, the ticket is blank save for the shiny gold finish. Then words begin to appear.

MISS EVE OLIVER is cordially invited to the Annual Winter Masquerade Ball hosted by Lord Nicholas Vanderbilt who looks forward to making your acquaintance.

ON THE BACK is a date and time but no location. "What's the significance of this ball?" I ask.

"Nothing," Liam says.

"Everything," Cole says at the same time. "It's the who's who of the Otherworld, and anybody who's anybody will be there. Lord Nicholas Vanderbilt is the Collector, and he will be having a secret auction that night where only a select view will be invited." Cole smiles at me. "If you attend, you could charm your way into that auction and see if he's got the egg."

"Why am I the only one who got an invitation?" I ask.

Derek shrugs. "You're a novelty, despite working for us. Meeting you is too enticing for him to pass up."

"Obviously I have to go, if there's a chance we could solve the case and save Liam," I say, glancing at the fire Druid, who doesn't make eye contact with me. Men are so mercurial, it's maddening.

"That's out of the question," Sebastian says. "We wouldn't be there to protect you, and anything could happen. The Collector is not one to mess with."

"I can escort her," Cole says. "If you're so worried about her safety."

Liam scoffs. "She's no safer with you. And besides, you didn't get a ticket."

Cole shrugs. "Very well, I'll keep my distance, but she should still go."

Before they can continue this argument, I clear my throat. "You all must be confused. I'm not asking for permission. I'm going to the ball. Alone. It's our biggest lead yet. And Cole is right. I can take care of myself."

I don't feel as confident as I sound about that last part, given my lack of control over my powers and my fears surrounding them, but this is the right decision, and they can suck it if they think they get to control what I do.

I smile charmingly. "I'd better go shopping for an outfit, then."

* * *

THE NIGHT OF THE BALL, Lily helps me dress. And given the complexity of the gown I'm wearing, I need all the help I can get.

It takes us—no lie—about four hours to get me ready. FOUR HOURS!?!?!? I'm so exhausted when we're done that I don't even want to go anymore, but Lily just laughs at me and spins me to face the mirror.

I gasp.

I look... magical.

The dress is Dryad inspired, made of shimmering emerald green fabric that curves around my body seductively, with slashes cut out to reveal my stomach and cleavage. Vines—that are magicked to look real and move on their own—wind up my legs and arms and twine around my gown dotted with white blossoms. My mask is made of diamonds and emeralds that are applied directly to my face directly, like makeup, so that I look as if I'm becoming a gemstone. The same stones dot my hair, which is twisted into elaborate braids intertwined with thin vines blossoming with more white flowers. My lips are blood red, my eyes are painted with sparkling silver, and the rest of my exposed skin is dusted with powdered diamond magicked to sparkle all night.

Lily drives me to our destination in the carriage, which has been recently cleaned, polished, and upgraded with deep cushions and a much better shock absorbing system. I have to remember to thank Elijah—and Liam, who very likely lit a fire under the air Druid's ass.

The horses are brushed down and wearing their most elaborate gear. We are quite the splendor, arriving as we do.

With a silly curtsy, Lily leaves me at the entrance and

escapes into the nearby trees to await my return. I stand before the grand double doors and take a nervous breath. I got this.

Straightening my back, I clench my ticket in my hand and ring the bell.

The doors immediately open, and an older man in a black tux, likely the butler, asks to see my ticket. I hand it to him, and he waves a hand inviting me in.

Inside the manor is a lavish display of wealth and luxury. Thousands of candles line the walls and tables, casting dancing light against the cream walls. Candelabras fall from the ceiling in intricate designs inspired by nature, creating haunting shadows on the ceiling. The ballroom has already attracted a crowd as an orchestra plays the most unusual instruments I've ever seen. A woman in the center, who seems the star, flicks the chords of what looks like a double-sided harp with the help of four extra arms.

The walls are lined with tables full of food and drink for all manner of supernatural creature. Vampires fill their goblets from the blood fountain. Mermaids in human form—their skin covered in the faintest trace of translucent scales—partake of the live seafood display. There's a table full of raw meat and small cages with live animals for the hunting carnivores. Wolves, maybe? I shiver and keep moving, making my way through the crowds, unsure of what I'm looking for.

I study the faces around me looking for a familiar one beneath the masks when I feel someone's breath against my neck, his body close to mine.

A hand lands on my ass as another wraps around my waist to graze my breast and I turn, shocked, to confront a man I don't recognize who wears a lewd expression.

"Get your hands off me!" I shout, pushing him back.

He's of medium build and height, with mousy brown hair and small, dark eyes. Honestly, he could be considered decent looking in another context, but right now I just want to cut off his hands.

He just smirks, tips his top hat at me, and walks away.

I'm so furious at the violation I'm shaking as my brain tries to catch up with my body. What do I do? Do I tell someone? This isn't the New York subway. I wasn't expecting such behavior, and it's triggering every vulnerable, angry, defiant feeling I've ever had when men take liberties as if my body is their personal toy.

The awful man walks across the room, his eyes clearly set on a young, green-haired mermaid enjoying live shrimp at one of the tables.

"Merde. You're the third woman I've seen him pull that shit on," a familiar voice whispers in my ear. His closeness makes me jump, and I spin on him, all my ire and rage welling up in me.

"What are you doing here?" I hiss, looking around to see if anyone noticed him.

And then I forget my words when I take a good look at the sexy dark Druid. He's dressed in all black, as per usual, with a long fur cape trimmed at the collar in black bird feathers. His mask is also made of feathers, and his hair is coifed in such a way that it changes his appearance entirely. I would swear on my life he's part bird if I didn't know better, and I squint at him, trying to see the magick I know is aiding his impressive illusion.

"Can you see it, then?" Cole asks, raising a hand to my

face and tracing my cheek gently. "Can you see the power that connects us?"

His dark eyes pull me in as always, and I shudder and step back, reluctantly fighting this attraction I feel. "I don't see anything," I say, but that's not entirely true, though 'see' might be the wrong word. I feel it, this tie, this thread that keeps pulling us closer together. But it scares me.

He tilts his head and smiles. "You will in time, *mon coeur*," he says softly. "What is here cannot be denied."

"You didn't answer my question, what are you doing here?"

"Disobeying my brothers, of course. And providing you with unnecessary backup. I couldn't resist the chance to see you in this gown, now could I?"

A clatter behind us pulls our attention to the table the mermaid was standing at. She drops her shrimp and flees the room with tears in her eyes, while the man grins broadly and no one steps in to do or say anything.

"He'll keep at it," Cole says. "No one will stop him."

I narrow my eyes. "Challenge accepted."

Cole grins and crosses his arms over his chest as I feel my power rise up in me. The wrath I feel, coupled with the fear and helplessness being grabbed brought up in me, makes it harder to access my power.

I close my eyes and take a deep breath, centering myself, then try again. This time, I am calm. I am cold. I am justice.

I call to the elements, and air floats up, but it brings with it the darkness, and when I dip into it, I get both elements in equal measure.

Each element I try to access also brings with it the

darkness, and I know there's no way around it, I have to let that power out, at least a little.

I open my eyes and watch as the man grabs a glass of something red to drink. I focus and flick my finger. The man's eyes widen as he stumbles, spilling the drink all over his suit. With another flick, I send him into a caged aquarium of piranhas. Or at least, sharp-tooth fish that look like piranhas. He breaks the tank as he falls, and fish latch on to him, drawing blood instantly as he screams for help.

Silence falls on the room as the rest of the guests just stand and stare. No one goes to his aid until the butler hurries in and helps escort the man out of the ballroom while other staff come in to contain the remaining fish and clean up the mess. Conversation resumes, the guests acting as if nothing has happened, and Cole gives me a sly wink and a subtle clap of admiration for my revenge. I must admit I feel pretty good about it, too.

As the musicians resume playing, Cole holds a hand out and offers me a charming grin. "Would the lady do me the honor of a dance?"

I'm tempted to say no, but I can't bring myself to do it. I want it too badly. So, I take his hand and let him guide me to the center of the dance floor.

The music changes tempo as if on cue, and Cole leads me in a passionate routine of complex steps that I've never done before. I'm convinced I'll fall flat on my face, but as he spins me and dips me and synchronizes his steps with mine, I find myself matching him step for step, as if we had practiced this hundreds of times. Our bodies move in time to each other, like planets orbiting one another. His body's pulse drives me, guides me, and it is as if no one exists but us. I can't feel anyone else in the room as he holds my lower back, pulling me against him, his lips brushing against my cheek.

Black tendrils of smoke seem to rise from him, and I feel his magick, his power, wrapping around me, touching and guiding me.

When the song ends, he pulls me into an embrace and dips me deeply.

That's when I realize the dance floor cleared for us, and then the crowd breaks into applause at our performance. I flush scarlet as Cole leads me away, his arm wrapped around my waist.

"How did you do that?" I ask, as we pause at a food table that tempts me with succulent roasted chicken, pasta salad, fruit platters, and pastries.

"We all have our talents," Cole says, in an answer that really isn't an answer at all.

We both fill a plate and get drinks, then move to the balcony to catch some fresh air. Unlike his brothers, the dark Druid is no vampire. He tastes like I taste. Feels like I feel.

"I'm glad you're here," I say, taking a bite of a chocolate covered strawberry.

We eat in silence for a few minutes, watching the Dragon's Breath float in the sky. Finally, I reluctantly pull away from him. "I have to go back in. I won't learn anything out here with you," I remind him.

He takes a step forward, his head dipping closer to mine, our lips inches apart. "Oh, you would learn plenty, mon coeur. I can promise you that."

"No doubt," I whisper, my voice thick. "But nothing about the egg." I'm desperately trying to hold onto my purpose for attending this event. Liam. I have to save Liam. But damn, Cole makes it hard to think sometimes.

"Then by all means, go collect clues. I'll be here when you're ready."

His words are layered with too many meanings for me to effectively unpack right now, so I turn and step back into the ballroom, and I walk right into someone I wasn't expecting to see, though it makes perfect sense that she would be here.

Lilith smiles at me, her teeth so white, her pale skin luminescent, her silky black hair falling down her back like a waterfall. She's wearing a pure white gown with a long trail, and a white feathered mask that flares up on the ends like cat eyes. Her lips are as red as mine and she looks enchanted. Beautiful. Dangerous.

"Can it be possible that you are here alone? Unaccompanied by the Night brothers?" she teases, handing me a glass of a foamy white drink with red sparkles in it.

I sip the drink and enjoy the frothy sweetness, but I know to be careful with supernatural alcohol. The magick packs a punch, so I drink slowly and cautiously. "They don't have me on a leash," I say, a little snippy.

"You must give those boys quite a run for their money," she says, grinning. "How marvelous." She links arms with me, and we move through the room. "What brings you here, then? You didn't strike me as the type to attend balls. Particularly alone."

I debate about how much to tell her. Our relationship —if one can call it that—is complicated. "Liam is being accused of conspiring to steal the dragon egg by starting the explosion at the Midwinter Festival. I'm here hoping to find anyone who might know something about what really happened," I say.

She raises an eyebrow. "I take it you do not believe he's responsible?"

"No, I don't," I say firmly.

She stares at me a moment, then nods. "I agree with you. This isn't Liam's style. But it is quite damning at the moment. I do hope you find what you're looking for. Wherever that might lead."

"Do you know anything?" I ask her point blank, not that I expect an honest answer. It's been my experience that the older and more powerful a supernatural being is, the more they enjoy speaking in goddamn riddles.

"I know you won't give up until you find the truth," she says. "And I know that tenacity puts you in the line of fire, no pun intended." She pulls away as someone across the room calls to her. "Be cautious," she says. "No one is who you think they are in this world. And nothing is as it seems."

Like I said. Riddles. She walks away with a final wink at me, and I realize I'm wasting precious time that I need in order to figure out how to get an invite into the secret auction later tonight.

I head to the bar in hopes of getting another drink and maybe some helpful information from the bar tender, but as I approach, a hand lands on my back. "Allow me," the tall man at my side says.

He's decked out in the richest velvet and finery, from his ring studded fingers to his tailored clothing, wealth oozing from him like pus from an infection. He looks to be in his 50s or 60s, with flecks of silver along his temples, and he has aristocratic features that give him—at first glance—a debonair style. But it's his eyes that tell me who he is before he does.

His eyes are dead. Soulless. All the charm in the world can't take the place of a soul.

He orders two drinks, both blood red, and hands me one. I eye it suspiciously and wait for him to drink first. When he does, I take a sip, relieved it's not blood or something equally awful.

It's bitter and strong, with a sweet aftertaste.

"Miss Eve Oliver," he says, with a drawl to his voice that belies his ruthlessness. "I am delighted you accepted my invitation. Allow me to introduce myself, I am—"

"Lord Nicholas Vanderbilt," I say, smiling my most charming smile. "It's a pleasure to meet you. Thank you for the invitation. This ball is extraordinary." At least I can be honest about that last part. It truly is exceptional.

I was never a very good actor. I tried out for a play in high school once. I got understudy but never had to actually perform, which is probably a good thing. But now I wish I'd studied it a little more seriously, because tonight will take all the acting skills I don't have to pull off feigning interest in this man who makes my skin crawl. As he cups my elbow and guides me through the crowd, a wave of nausea crashes through me and I set my drink down on a nearby table.

"Was it not to your liking?" he asks, eyeing the nearly full glass that's left.

"It was lovely," I say, smiling. "I'm just pacing myself."

He nods, a glint in his eyes. "A woman of temperance. I appreciate that. It's lacking in most who prefer wild extremes."

"And you?" I ask. "Are you a temperate man or one of extremes?"

I study him, and for all intents he looks human. I wonder at his supernatural race. He must have one, to be here.

"I am a man of cultivated tastes and specific desires," he says enigmatically.

The door to the ballroom opens, distracting us both as we glance over at the newcomer. A tall man with fire red hair that flows down his back walks in. He wears a red cloak that looks to be made of a strange material, and his eyes…his eyes…

The Collector smiles and escorts me to the man, who, as we get closer, I realize isn't a man at all.

"Miss Oliver, you have met Dath'Racul before, yes? I believe in his true form."

The fire dragon looks at me, eyes narrowing, and I smile nervously and hold out a hand, unsure what the proper protocol. "Yes. You were the judge at Dracula's trial," I say.

He studies my hand but does not shake it, and I awkwardly let it drop to my side.

"Indeed. You had quite the last-minute turnabout," he says, his voice as deep as it was in dragon form.

As a man, he is beautiful. His golden dragon eyes study everything around us with keen intelligence, and what I thought was a cape is actually his wings, draped around him. His skin is a deep burnt red and his body is massive for a man. Though I imagine he feels small in this form, compared to being a dragon.

"I am surprised to see you here," Dath'Racul says to me, then glances curiously at the Collector.

"It was a pleasant surprise for us all," Nicholas says. "What a rare jewel to grace our presence."

I stifle a shudder at his strange praise, knowing from rumor how he likes to collect 'rare jewels.'

"I would think Miss Oliver would have better things to do, with the trial against her employer so imminent," the dragon says with cold arrogance. "Certainly, Mr. Night is hoping for more commitment to the preparation,"

Oh boy, this guy is really trying to get my goat.

But I won't let him.

"Rest assured, The Night Firm is doing everything in its power to prove that Liam is innocent. We have many other leads that are much more damning than Liam being in the same location as everyone else in town at the time of the explosion. That seems a pretty weak foundation to prove guilt, don't you think?" I ask the judge.

He frowns. "Not many can conjure that kind of fire."

"I don't know about this world, but in my world, us talking specifics about the case like this would be justification for change of venue. Or at least a new judge," I say with another disarming smile. Honestly, after tonight, I may never smile again. My teeth hurt from exposing them to so much slime.

Dath'Racul nods. "Of course. You are correct. But you must not have heard; I am not the judge on this case."

Finally, good news, but his cruel smile doesn't encourage me.

"I will be prosecuting the case against Mr. Night," Dath'Racul says.

Shit. Shit, shit and double effing shit. How can this even be allowed? I have to keep my cool. "I think you mean you'll be prosecuting the case against the person ultimately found responsible? Surely you are committed to justice? To exploring all leads? There have been rumors of conflict with the people of the Otherworld and the dragon leadership. It's a promising lead that might exonerate Liam by pointing the finger at the true guilty party."

I study his face as he responds to my veiled threat.

"I am sure you will find the answer is not nearly so simple. It is natural that a society would want to challenge its leaders. They do not have all the information and thus question decisions they do not understand," he says.

"Perhaps it's time they had all the information then," I say.

His face hardens, but before he can say more, Nicholas chuckles. "It's good to see you, Dath'Racul. Get a drink and enjoy the party. I'd like to show Eve off to a few more people before the night escapes us."

Dath'Racul nods curtly and walks away, grabbing a flaming fire drink from a tray carried by a beautiful woman with cat ears and a tail. She is wearing almost nothing save a see-through white body suit studded with diamonds. The same as all the young, female servers. Her eyes are large and cat-like, and her pale white hair falls down her back in waves. She locks eyes with me, and though she smiles, I see the pain in them and wonder about her story. About why she's here.

Nicholas escorts me around, introducing me to the rich and powerfully corrupt of the Otherworld. I try to be charming and smile and engage in harmless conversation. The effort is exhausting, and I find myself looking around to catch a glimpse of Cole, but he seems to have disappeared. I wish he were closer. I may not need backup, but I could use the moral support in this den of vipers.

The band begins to play a new song and Nicholas holds out his hand and bows gallantly. "May I have this dance, Miss Oliver?"

"Of course," I say, through the most insincere smile I've ever worn. How can he not see how uncomfortable I am? Or does he only see what he wants to? Maybe he's the kind of man who can't conceive of anyone finding him repulsive, so it never enters his mind that someone might not enjoy his company. I've known a few of those types in my life and most of them weren't even paranormal.

It's a slow dance, of course, and his hand slides too low down my back, making me very uncomfortable. But I'm here for answers, so I don't pull away.

As he spins me and guides me over the dance floor, his gaze locks on mine. "You are a very beautiful woman," he says.

"Thank you."

My hands are sweating, but there' nothing I can do about the one he's holding. My other hand is on his waist.

"Word has it you are human. At least, that was the story when you first got here."

There's no question so I keep silent, waiting for him to continue.

"It is clear to me you are not human at all. But then, what are you? Pray do tell. I have been dying to find out for some time."

"I don't actually know," I say truthfully. "I always thought I was human as well."

He laughs. "Playing hard to get, I see. Very well, I enjoy games more than most. What would you like in exchange for this knowledge about you?"

His question surprises me. "What do you mean?" I ask.

He plunges me into a dip, our legs pressing against each other as he does, then pulls me back up to face him, our bodies entirely too close. I finally see Cole in the background, watching us. He winks when he sees me staring.

"I mean," says Nicholas, spinning me so I no longer see the Night brother, "that I am willing to play this game and offer you all manner of treasure in exchange for your secret."

"I really can't tell you," I say.

He studies me quietly for a moment. "With anyone else, I would offer wealth. Jewels. The power of my influence. But with you..." he ponders as we continue moving in synch. "With you, I feel you value more significant trades. Perhaps you would part with your secret for information about the dragon egg you are seeking."

I glance up in surprise. "Do you know where the egg is?" I ask.

"I could find information about its location, if we have an agreement."

I frown. "You're really not listening," I say. "I don't know what I am. I swear. But if you have information about the egg, maybe we could discuss another trade?"

"You're an intriguing woman, Miss Oliver. You effectively punished a man who was causing problems for the women at my party, for which I thank you. And I apologize that you were made to suffer such indignities."

"I don't know what you mean," I say, but he knows I'm lying, I can tell.

"Indeed." He pushes his hips closer to mine and I can feel his attraction to me, and it makes me sick. "I also saw you talking with Lilith, Mother of all Vampires. You keep interesting company."

"I could say the same of you," I say, looking around.

"Touché," he says with a chuckle. "What will it take for you to trust me?"

I shrug. "I don't trust easily. Don't take offense. It's the foster kid in me."

A smile curls at his lip as the orchestra completes its song. "Thank you for the dance. I have another—more private—event to introduce in the basement. Would you care to join me? You will find a great deal that might interest you."

This is it. This is what the whole night has been about. But I can't let myself look too excited. Play it cool, Eve. You got this.

"Sounds intriguing, but I don't typically follow strange men into basements. Another foster kid thing. You understand."

I make to walk away from him, but he grabs my hand to stop me. "You will be in no danger, and there will be other select guests in attendance. I give you my word you will be safe."

I turn back to him and smile. "Very well. I'd be honored to be your guest."

THE BIDDING

I am darkness A moonless night Grasping for stars Any trace of light The thunder resounding The lightning will transform I am the whirlwind I am the storm ~Jennifer Borak

As Nicholas escorts me out of the ballroom, I see Cole watching us, his gaze burning a hole in my back until we disappear from his sight. And even still, I can feel him close to me, his presence lingering.

We walk down a long corridor that ends at a door, behind which is a circular stairway that winds its way down quite a distance. We take the stairs quickly, and my shoes clack on the stone as we walk in silence, with just magically lit torches on the gray walls to light our way.

When we reach the bottom, he opens another door, and a bouncer dressed in black greets us with a nod. He's shaped like a boulder, round and solid, and looks ready to rumble with anyone who breaks the rules.

When we reach the end of the hall, the Collector pulls

away from me. "This is where I must leave you for now, to attend to my duties. Please, enjoy yourself and explore. The activities will begin shortly."

Once alone, I look around the large room with hand-painted tile flooring and white walls with murals depicting enchanting magical scenes of mermaids and dryads and dragons. An incredible chandelier hangs from the ceiling and white velvet chairs are lined up in rows.

A woman with wild curly blue hair and scales covering her skin hands me a crystal. "This projects your bid number for the auction. Hold out your hand, please."

I do as she says, and she pricks my thumb with a different crystal. "Miss Eve Oliver with The Night Firm. You are officially registered. Best of luck."

I rub my sore thumb and take a moment to look around. As I wander down a long hall, I notice doors spaced a few feet apart, and I hear the sounds of sex from within several of them.

One door opens and a man comes out buttoning his pants. Behind him I see the server I noticed upstairs, the cat girl, laying on the bed naked, her eyes empty, her smile a mask to cover her pain.

Are these women here of their own accord? Something feels off.

Another man pushes past me into the room, and the woman stands and closes the door, her eyes flicking to mine before she does.

I want to speak to her, to ask her about this life she's living, but there is no opportunity, so I walk back to the main room where other women are carrying trays around serving hors d'oeuvres and drinks. I take something a glass of champagne and sip at it, then find a seat. Weariness settles over me and I wish I could just go home. But I'm finally getting closer to actual answers. I can't give up now.

Someone sits next to me and I see it's Lilith, holding her own crystal.

"So, you have made your way into the secret den," she says, softly. "Be careful not to get in over your head. You may not be human, but you've led a very short human life that has not prepared you for this world."

Our conversation is cut short when Nicholas takes the stage and addresses the crowd. The chairs are now full and everyone looks eager to see what will be up for auction tonight.

"We have five very special treats for you this evening," he says, charm oozing out of him. "So, without further ado, let us begin."

There is a chorus of clapping as Nicholas snaps his fingers and in a puff of smoke an ebony box appears on the stage, centered on a table. It's about the size of a bread box and covered in intricate carvings. It's also wrapped in iron chains and has a lock that glows blue and pulses with some kind of runes.

"You've heard of Pandora's Box," Nicholas says, smiling. "A myth, of course, but not without basis in truth. This is the origin of that myth. The original holder of darkness. Open this at your own peril, for only you will be affected. It will give you the power of the dark, but at a steep price. Can I get an opening bid?"

I stare at the box curiously as those around me bid aggressively. What would happen to me if I opened it? Would it corrupt me? Or am I already corrupted? What would it do to Adam, I wonder?

When the winning bid has been announced, the item disappears into smoke to be replaced by something new.

A gold necklace lying against black velvet. It is beautifully wrought in the shape of two serpents with open mouths that form a clasp in the front. The gold itself is studded with emeralds and diamonds that twinkle under the lights of the chandelier. It's a breathtaking piece.

"Behold the Necklace of Harmonia," the Collector says. "Anyone who wears this necklace will be granted eternal youth and beauty. But at a cost. Legend says this necklace brings great misfortune to all who wear it. Is it worth the trade? Let the bidding begin."

"Fools," Lilith says, as the bidding ensues. "They will beg to be released from the curse of that bauble before long. I have seen it happen too many times. There are better ways to attain eternal youth and beauty. Though none without a price, 'tis true."

A beautiful, slim man with raven hair and reptilian eyes wins the necklace and preens like a peacock at his prize. I wonder what tragedy will befall him should he chose to wear the cursed jewelry.

Once again, it disappears into smoke and a marble stand appears with a large tome atop it. The book is bound in leather and stamped with the symbol of a crescent moon lying on its side with a circle above it.

Next to me, Lilith straightens her back and leans forward, clutching her crystal. It appears something has caught the vampire's interest.

"Many of you have come for this treasure this evening," Nicholas says. "I expect some animated bidding for the Book of Thoth, a text said to have been written by Thoth himself, the Egyptian god of writing and knowledge. Whether he actually existed or not, this manuscript contains powerful spells and knowledge found nowhere else in either world. Though many such books were said to have existed, this is the last of its kind. Shall we start the bidding?"

Lilith raises her crystal and a holographic number displays before her as she calls out the first bid. After that, the competition is fierce and the price climbs higher than anything that came before it.

In the end, no one wanted it more than the mother of vampires herself, and though she spends a small fortune, she clearly feels it's worth it.

"This is what I came for," she says, softly. "The greatest power in either of our worlds is knowledge. Remember that."

My curiosity is piqued, and for a moment I consider asking Lilith to see the book, but then the fourth 'item' up for auction appears and my blood runs cold.

I shift uncomfortably in my seat and don't know where to look or how to behave. This isn't what I was expecting, and I feel sick to my stomach. How can I remain silent? But what can I possibly do?

Lilith notices my distress and puts a hand on my knee. "Do not play your cards just yet, my dear. This isn't the fight you came here for."

She's not wrong, but holy hell how am I supposed to keep quiet?

This auction item isn't a cursed necklace or powerful book or box.

It's a young woman.

With cat ears.

The one who served drinks upstairs and served herself down here.

Now she is being sold to the highest bidder.

The Collector traffics in people.

Alive people.

Not just trinkets and dead body parts.

No one prepared me for this.

"Feast your eyes on the splendor of this beauty," Nicholas says, displaying the girl like a piece of art. She is once again in her see-through body suit, her face neutral, her white tail twitching nervously behind her.

"Many of you have tasted of her rare pleasures. Now, she can be yours forever. Let the bidding begin."

The girl looks at me, and I can't pull my gaze from her as mostly men—but also some women—bid to own her. I can only imagine the things they will do to her.

I break eye contact with her to glance at Lilith, who is impassive in the face of this atrocity. "Please do something," I say, feeling helpless even as my powers roil beneath the surface of my skin. I could unleash them here, but then I would ruin everything. What if the egg is the last up for auction? But how can I ignore what's happening?

Lilith looks at me with unreadable eyes, then gives a brief nod and holds up her crystal, entering into the bidding.

I scoot to the edge of my chair, desperate for her to win and free the girl.

Another man in the audience outbids Lilith at every turn.

She's starting to look pissed.

"Please keep going," I say. "You can't let him have her."

"Oh, I won't," she seethes between her teeth.

When the price becomes more than my mind can compute, Lilith stands up and bids an even higher amount, then takes off a ring she's wearing, holding it up for Nicholas. "I also offer the Ring of Dispel as payment. A one-of-a-kind wonder that, when worn, dispels any enchantments. It's said to have been given to Sir Lancelot by the Lady of the Lake. I can attest to its power."

The man who had been bidding against her huffs. "That's not right. She can't do that," he complains, his lusty eyes consuming the poor girl on stage.

Nicholas can't take his gaze off the ring, and I can see how badly he wants it. "Agreed," he says to Lilith, who hands over the ring with a shrewd glance at me.

The other man storms out of the room, and the cat girl looks to me and Lilith in curiosity and fear. Likely, she is wondering what will become of her.

The girl looks at me, eyes wide, before Nicholas snaps and she disappears. "Done." He slips the coveted ring onto his finger and smiles.

"You will free her, yes?" I ask Lilith.

Lilith looks at me. "I will do something with her."

I frown. "What does that mean?"

"It means, the girl probably doesn't have anywhere to go once she's freed. But I'll sort it out." She rolls her eyes at me. "You have a soft heart, Eve. Don't let it get you killed."

"And for our last—and truly most incredible—item for auction, behold the wonder that is the Viden," the Collector says and waves his hand with a flourish. From out of the mist appears a greyish-green creature at least ten feet in length pinned to a stone slab. It has a face like a deep-sea fish and the body of a snake, dozens of tentacles sprouting from its sides.

"This magnificent being can read into the hearts and minds of any being to answer their most burning questions. But the truth isn't always what it appears to be," the Collector cautions. "Captured from the deep seas near the edge of the world, the Viden is said to be the last of its kind. Who would like to volunteer to demonstrate its powers?"

Several hands go up, but I just stare as the creature's black, beady eyes lock onto mine, and I feel the pull of the darkness within it, as if it is calling my name.

Eve.

Eve.

Eve.

Lilith nudges me, snapping me out of the trance I was in without realizing. "What's going on?" I ask.

Everyone in the room is looking at me, and the Collector is holding out his hand to me. "Miss Oliver, would you join me on stage?"

I want to say no, but if this creature can answer my questions, maybe it's worth it.

I reluctantly stand and make my way forward, then take the seat in the chair provided, directly in front of the creature.

"The Viden will answer any three questions you have. Are you ready?" Nicholas asks.

I nod and prepare myself for whatever is about to happen.

But nothing can prepare me for the creature being released from the stone slab and crawling over my head, covering my face with its body, wrapping around me until I can't breathe.

Invisible cuffs hold me to the chair, and I try to scream but nothing comes out.

Fear takes hold of me and I pull out my power, but nothing happens.

The creature's voice fills my mind.

Eveeeeeeeee, you have questions for me. What are they, Eveeeeeeee?

I can't speak, but as I think my first question, the creature seems to understand. And though I can't breathe, somehow I do not run out of air.

Where is the missing dragon egg? I think.

The creature hums in my head as if searching for the answer.

It is nearer than you know but farther than you are. Seek it in the place you will be, when your world is about to crumble.

Of course. Of course, the answers would just be more riddles.

Next question Eveeee. I cannot release you until you ask all three.

What am I?

It seems amused.

Delightful and doubtful and despairing of truth. You are all of them and more and none of them in lore. You cannot be hidden or brought out. You are the answer and the question.

For the love of all that's holy, I'm so tired of this. Okay, I get one last question. Maybe a yes or no will give me a clearer response, though I'm not optimistic.

Is my brother evil?

The creature sniffs. *Evil is as evil does. Does motive or*

madness matter? Do ends and beginnings tell the same story? Nothing is at it appears. Least of all, fate's twins.

And with the last question, the creature removes itself from my head, leaving me sticky with its tentacle goo, which has completely destroyed my mask and costume.

Nicholas notices my disheveled state and waves his hand over me. In a rush of magic, the goo disappears, and my costume is restored. He reaches for my hand to help me to my feet, and though I don't want to touch him, I'm too unsteady to rise on my own.

"Well, my dear, did you get the answers you were hoping for?"

His grin is maddening. He knew what kind of response I would get from the Viden, but I don't want to play his game. "Oh yes. It was most illuminating. Particularly in relation to what I am," I whisper.

He flinches, stepping back.

Dizziness overtakes me as I attempt to walk back to my chair, and Lilith steadies me and guides me out of the auction room and through a door leading outside. Once there, Cole greets us.

"What happened to her?" he asks, lifting me into his arms when I sway and nearly fall.

"Nicholas punished her in his own way," Lilith says.

Cole growls under his breath, and the feel of his chest rumbling is soothing to me. My head flops against his torso and the world fades in and out.

When darkness takes me, it is Cole's darkness that I feel. Cole's that I fall into blissfully, forgetting all the horrors of the night.

I regain my consciousness—and my memory of the evening—several hours later and wake to find myself in front of a fireplace in the library, a knitted blanket covering me. Matilda is crocheting in the chair across from me and smiles when I wake. "Welcome back," she says. "You've had quite the adventure."

I sit up, clutching my head as I do to keep it from rolling off my shoulders or exploding.

"There's a potion for you to drink," she says. "It will help."

I see a mug on the table before me and pick it up, sniffing. "Ugh. What is this?" I ask, crinkling my nose.

"Something that will remove the demon you brought home within you," she says nonchalantly, as if commenting about a headache.

"Demon?"

She nods. "Oh yes. He's hitched a ride and needs to head back to where he belongs now. Drink up."

I take the vile liquid in like I'm doing the longest, worst-tasting shot in the history of shots. And then my body convulses, and I see a bucket next to the couch that I grab to vomit into.

The vomiting seems to last days, but it doesn't faze Matilda.

When there's nothing left in me, I look into the bucket and see that's it's all black sludge.

She sets her crocheting down and comes to me, feeling my head and examining the bucket. Then she says some words and does a symbol above the sludge, and it all disappears.

"There. All gone. How do you feel?"

Like shit. But also…"a bit better. My mind isn't as muddled."

"Sounds like you had an interesting evening," she says.

"That's one word for it," I say. "I... think I need to go to bed. And brush my teeth. My mouth tastes like demon."

Matilda nods, as if this is all par for the course. "Sleep well, dear. You'll feel much better in the morning."

My body aches and I feel exactly as one might expect to feel after having a demon exorcised from their body. I do as promised and scrub my mouth clean until I can only remember the taste of vomiting up demon.

Then I try to undress. Holy shit. It takes me forever to figure out how to undo all the pieces of my gown, and once I'm naked I soak in a hot bathtub for a long time, letting the warmth melt away all my aches.

But a bath can't help the pain in my heart.

There were other girls there that night who were likely owned by Nicholas. Other girls he will abuse and sell and trade. I can't leave them there, but what can I do? How can I fix this?

I close my eyes, trying to sort through it all, when someone very close to me clears their throat.

I startle and look up to see Cole standing at the edge of my bath with a half-smile on his face.

"If I wasn't here on very important business I would be so tempted to ask if I could join you."

His words light up something inside of me, and I wonder what it would feel like to have him in the bath with me, to feel his skin against mine, our bodies becoming one.

I shake my head to dispel those thoughts. "What are you doing here?" I ask.

"I have a surprise for you," he says. "But you have to come with me."

"Right now?" I ask.

He nods. "It'll be worth it, I promise."

There's something in his eyes that convinces me it's worth going, so I stand up and his eyes take in my body as he hands me a towel. I dry and dress as quickly as I can, despite needing sleep very badly. "Where are we going?" I ask.

"Not far."

He takes my hand and pulls me into his arms. "Do you trust me?" he asks.

I look into his too-dark eyes and nod, because for some reason, despite everything, I do.

"Then close your eyes and hold on tight."

I do as I'm told, and with our bodies pressed together, I feel his power move through me, and then...it's as if for a moment we are in another realm made of air and smoke and shadow. And then I feel solid again and I'm standing in a room made of stone. A thin sheen of dust covers the walls, telling me that no one has been here for some time. A door to my right leads...somewhere. From the window I can see the top of the castle and the surrounding grounds. "Are we in the eastern tower?" I ask.

Cole nods.

And when I turn, I see what his surprise is.

Nicholas Vanderbilt is slumped in the corner, tied up, blindfolded and gagged.

"What is this?" I ask.

"A gift," Cole says. "He tortured you with that creature, sent you home demon possessed, and sells girls as sex slaves. He deserves to be punished. I thought you might like to do the honors."

I step forward, looking at the man who does indeed deserve a thousand cuts with the sharpest blade. My anger flares within me and fire appears in my palms. I hold my hands up, studying the flames. I could release them on his flesh. Burn him alive. Make him pay for all he's done.

"Can he hear us?" I ask.

"No," Cole says. "Would you like him to?"

I shake my head. I don't know what I want right now.

Cole comes up behind me, his mouth at my ear. "It will feel so good to unleash your magic on him. And he deserves it, doesn't he?"

"Your brothers wouldn't like this," I say, holding my fiery hands in front of me, visualizing the Collector burning alive.

"My brothers don't understand many things. They are limited by their own self-imposed rules. You should not be bound by those."

The temptation overwhelms me. I could so easily do it. Who would know?

"What happened to the girls he held prisoner?" I ask.

"They are free to live their own lives."

I turn to face him. "You rescued them?"

He nods, brushing a lock of hair from my face gently. "Of course."

He leans down and kisses me softly, the act sending shivers up my spine. His kiss deepens and I melt into him, into the darkness he cocoons me in like a warm blanket on a winter night.

When I pull away, he sighs, closing his eyes and flicking his tongue over his lips. "You taste as I imagined you would."

When his eyes open, they are luminous. "Eve. Do you have any idea what you and I could do together? Who we could be with one another?"

I don't answer, but I can feel it, and I want it. So bad.

But...

Shit.

I drop my hands.

"I can't. I can't be that person." I turn to Nicholas. "And he doesn't deserve a quick death. He deserves to pay for his crimes. We must tell your brothers and let them turn Nicholas over to the Enforcers. The girls you freed will testify against him. He will finally get the justice he deserves."

"As you wish," Cole says sadly. "But it will not end the way you hope."

THE DARKNESS

The dance between darkness and light will always remain— the stars and the moon will always need the darkness to be seen, the darkness will just not be worth having without the moon and the stars. ~C. JoyBell C.

IN MY ROOM later that night, I find myself in a restless state despite my exhaustion. After hours of pacing, I sit on the patio and watch the Dragon's Breath dancing in the sky as I consider whether I made the right choice.

Will the Collector get justice? Will justice be enough? Will he have a chance to harm others in the meantime? Should I have killed him when I had the chance?

Derek wasn't happy that Cole had brought him here, but the Enforcers came and arrested the Collector based on my statement of his illegal activity. Cole didn't say another word about it, but I could see on his face that he felt this plan was doomed to failure.

He might not be wrong, but just because I might fail doesn't mean I didn't make the morally right choice.

So why do I feel so hallow?

"Why so glum, sis?"

I whip around, the voice behind me startling me out of my thoughts. "Adam?"

I stand, my heart fluttering at the sight of him. I still can't believe he's back. He's alive.

He reaches over and hugs me, and I smile into his shoulder, despite everything, then I guide him to the chairs in front of the fire. "How did you get in here?" I ask.

"Magic," he says, with a flourish of his hands and a chuckle. He leans in and takes my hands. "You're so much more powerful than you realize, Evie. You have no idea." He studies my palms as if they might give him the answers to my powers, but he says nothing about what he sees. Then he pulls back and leans against the chair, crossing his left leg over his right. He used to cross his right over his left, I realize. It's a stupid observation to make, but it strikes me there is a lot about my brother I no longer know. And a lot about me he doesn't know. This is the longest we've ever spent apart from each other, and our experiences since his—well, death—have shaped us each differently.

"I have something for you," he says, pulling a small package from his cloak and handing it to me.

It's wrapped in a blue silk cloth and tied with a silver ribbon. "What's this for?" I ask.

"It's my Christmas gift to you," he says. "Or, Midwinter gift, I guess. You seem to have acclimated to this new world quite well."

His words aren't accusatory at all, just an observation,

and yet I feel the sting of them just the same. What does it say about me that I was able to slough off my old life without a glance backwards?

Still, I unwrap his gift and find a small velvet box. Within is a stunning silver ring with a shiny black stone in the center in the shape of a rectangle, and red stones on either side.

"It's black onyx," he says. "It will protect you."

I slide the ring onto my finger and I actually feel a shift in the air around me, like a barrier forming. "This is so strange," I say, my mind drifting. "I had a dream about this ring. I'd forgotten it but it's all come back to me now. I found a ring just like this in a marsh surrounded by ancient trees." I look up at my brother. "It's uncanny that you would get this for me."

"We're twins," he says with a shrug. "We've always had an uncanny connection, don't you think?"

"Yes, of course, you're right." I shake off the feeling of unease with the memory of all the times our lives interconnected in strange ways. We often had the same dreams or nightmares...sometimes we'd even appear in each other's. The next day we'd remember what we did in the other person's dreams. I haven't thought about that in so long, and the memory causes an ache in my heart.

Tears fill my eyes and I reach over and grab his hand. "I've missed you." I sniff, then swipe at my eyes with my free hand. "Your remains are still on my mantelpiece."

He laughs and glances up at them, just above the fireplace. "I noticed. But you don't have to miss me anymore. I'm right here."

Then he stands, a small, sad smile on his lips. "And I will be back," he promises. "But for now, I have to go."

I stand and hug him again. "Why?"

"You know why. If I'm found here, the truth will come out about who really killed Mary and her baby and I'll be arrested. I can't risk it when there's so much to do."

"We have to talk soon," I say. "I'm having a hard time wrapping my mind around the moral conundrum you've created."

He kisses my forehead. "We will. For now, keep that ring on and be careful. I love you, Evie."

"I love you, too," I say, but before my sentence is out, he's gone. He hopped over the balcony and seemed to vanish into nothing.

A moment later there's a knock on my door and my heart beats so hard in my chest it feels like it's going to crack a rib.

If it's Liam... if he heard anything, that will put me in a sticky situation. He needs to be focused on himself. On the case that could end his freedom for good if he's convicted. Finding out the truth about Mary and my brother's roll in her death could be a fatal distraction for him. I tell myself I'm keeping this from him for his own good, but, of course, I also have selfish motives. I don't want to hurt him. I don't want to lose him. What if, once he finds out, he sees my brother every time he looks at me?

But when I pull open the door, it's not Liam standing there.

It's Cole.

"Bonsoir, Eve," he says, with a gallant bow. "I hope I'm not disturbing you." He glances behind me and frowns. "I thought I heard you talking to someone."

I try to look as innocent as possible. "No. I mean, I

sometimes talk aloud to myself." I shrug as if this is totally normal.

He grins. "Did you know one of the gifts of working with the darkness is the ability to tell if someone is lying?"

Well, shit. "No, I didn't. But I thought you were a light Druid?"

I hold the door open, letting him in, and we both sit in front of the fire, where Adam and I had just been sitting.

"I was. But I found that light without darkness is an imbalance of nature. I wasn't utilizing my power to its fullest potential, limiting myself to just the one element. Once I opened myself to darkness, I grew more than you can imagine."

I frown. "So now you're a lie detector?"

He nods.

"That would be handy," I say, thinking of the ways I could make good use of that skill. With clients. With witnesses. With my personal life.

And then I wonder, is this his way of telling me he heard me and my brother talking? Should I ask? Ignore it? I'm not good at this subterfuge shit.

"I am not my brothers," he says. "Yes, I heard you and your brother talking. I heard what he did. And I do not judge. I believe we have to do the wrong things for the right reasons sometimes."

"Like killing an evil priest and his followers?" I ask softly.

He gazes at the fire and nods slowly. "Yes, like that. But that wasn't the first time I killed," he says.

I wait to see if he wants to share more.

"When I lived in France, my master, he was indeed a great teacher. I learned a lot from him." Cole pauses, and I feel his energy shift. "He was also a rapist. And I was his preferred target."

Oh god. No.

Cole looks at me, his dark eyes so intense. "I killed him with my magic one night when I couldn't take it anymore. That's how I found the darkness. That night."

He pauses, searching my face.

His story tears me apart, and I can only imagine the vast pain he's suffered, first as a child, then as a man when his brothers imprisoned him. What horror he has been dealt. What tragedy.

"I had to go to great lengths to acquire my power," he says, studying me. "But you have only to tap into what is already within you." He leans forward. "I can teach you."

My heart skips a beat and my palms become slick with sweat. I can feel the darkness below the other elements, lurking like a hungry beast waiting for its moment to strike. I pull back, looking away. "I can't. It's too risky."

"You have been so afraid of your darkness that you're stifling your light," Cole says, his dark gaze probing into me until I can't help but look back at him.

I wonder…is this why my brother is so much stronger than me? He's tapping into his darkness in ways I have been unwilling to? But at what cost?

"Isn't it reasonable to be scared of what I'm capable of?" I ask. "To fear hurting others? To be wary of this dark cancer that's in danger of consuming me?"

He brushes a lock of hair off my face, his fingers creating a trail of fire over my skin. "Only if you believe in the lie of duality. In the falsehood of either/or. I don't," he says frankly. "There's a verse in a religious text that says, 'The light shines in the darkness and the darkness has not overcome it.' And that is true. But what they don't say is that the light hasn't overcome the darkness either." He holds up his hand, palm facing me, and takes mine, placing it against his. His skin is warm and reassuring. "We are the light and the darkness. The two seeming dualities that need each other to be in balance. It is light, after all, that creates life's shadows. And it is the embrace of darkness that makes the light shine brightest."

Tears burn my eyes as I look at our hands pressed against each other. I can feel his power pulsing under his skin. I can see it in his black eyes, in the shadows that move within them. It is a dark magic, a magic practiced under the cover of night, but it is not evil. He is not evil. And maybe, neither am I. Despite what I've done, and what I might still do.

"Eve," he says softly. "You are the light to my darkness and I am the darkness to your light. We have pieces of each other within ourselves, and that is what makes us stronger together. If you can surrender to that, there's nothing you can't do."

He twines his fingers through mine and pulls us both to standing position, then bridges the gap between us. He dips his head and leans in, his lips brushing against my ear. "I need you," he says. "More than I've ever needed anything."

"You have me," I say. Because I'm done fighting this. I'm done fighting myself and my own nature. I'm done fighting him.

I am complete with him.

My light and darkness in balance.

No longer at war with each other.

"I'm not like my brothers," he says again, as he pulls his

hand out of mine to wrap them around my waist. "I don't crave your blood, but I do crave your soul. You're light." He gently kisses my neck, sending shivers up my spine. "And your darkness. I want it all. I can handle it all."

I suck in my breath as a fire is lit in my belly. Need and desire crash into me, and I am consumed with them. With him.

When his lips make their way to mine, it is with slow deliberation, the passion contained in feather-light kisses that leave me breathless and desperate for more. He drops his hands to my hips and presses himself against me.

An ache grows in me and our kisses deepen.

My nails dig into his back, pressing through his shirt as I cling to him. When he pulls away, I groan, my body missing his.

"Do you trust me?" he asks.

I nod and allow him to lead me to the bed.

He undresses me slowly, meticulously, his dark eyes locked on me, his hands caressing every inch of me with such tenderness and devotion I nearly melt.

I feel no embarrassment as I stand before him naked. "You have too many clothes on," I remind him.

He strips quickly and my breath catches at the beauty of his body, perfect in every way, despite the scars he lives with. Or maybe because of them. After all, it's often our imperfections that give us our real beauty, and he is a beautiful man, with his long fingers, hard lines and sharply defined muscles.

With shocking ease, he lifts me into his arms and lays me on the bed, then produces strips of black silk cloth.

I don't resist as he ties one cloth around my eyes,

rendering me blind, and then gently ties each of my wrists to the bedposts.

"Surrender to the darkness," he whispers against my flesh, his lips and hands teasing me in all the most sensitive places.

I nod, unable to speak, as I lose myself in the sensations he's coaxing from me.

When he spreads my legs and teases my sex with his tongue I nearly lose myself, but he pulls back, unwilling to let me finish so quickly.

He takes his time with my body, and as I writhe under his merciless teasing, something happens I have never experienced before. The lines between us dissipate. The boundaries of flesh give way to a complete melding of his spirit and mine. I feel him everywhere, on every inch of my body, within me, caressing me and kissing me in ways that can't be possible with just one human body.

When I can no longer hold back, he undoes the ties restraining me and blinding me, and I see a black mist mixed with gold that has become a part of both of us. We are no longer two entities, but one, and when I climax, he is in me, riding the wave with me, our bodies wrapped into each other, the light and the dark becoming one.

THE SECRET

I will love the light for it shows me the way, yet I will endure the darkness for it shows me the stars. ~Og Mandino

MATILDA IS SITTING in front of her fire knitting when she calls for me to enter and have a seat. There's already a steaming cup of tea waiting for me.

How does she always know?

I curl up in the overstuffed leather chair and sip at my drink as we sit in silence for a few moments.

"I can hear your mind spinning, my dear. What have you come to ask?" She smiles at me kindly, then returns her attention to the sweater she's working on.

"I used to think that right and wrong were very clear cut," I say. "But recently...with my growing powers and other things that have happened, I'm starting to wonder about that."

Matilda pauses, laying her hands on her lap, and looks deeply into the fire. "This is about Cole," she says.

"He's in my bed as we speak," I confess. After we made love, he fell asleep, but my mind was too restless. It was hard to leave his warm body for the chilly hallways of the castle, but I needed to clear my head. To talk to someone who might understand.

She glances at me, a small smile on her lips. "He is not as evil as some of his brothers might like to believe," she says. "I've known those boys their whole lives, and I can tell you that they have all done the wrong thing for right reason, and the right thing for the wrong reason, more times than I can count. In other words, they are all more human than they fancy themselves to be. You cannot live as long as they have and not pick up a few demons along the way. It's what we do about our demons that define us. And that definition isn't static. It changes with each choice we make, with each path we choose. We are, none of us, beyond redemption or beyond change. But the longer we follow the dark path, the harder it becomes to choose the light."

"So, Cole has done evil things?" I ask.

She shrugs. "I suppose it depends on how you define evil. Many religions would argue that disobedience against their god or their god's laws is evil. But then great suffering has been wrought by those very same religions. One could conceivably argue that they perpetrated more evil than they cured. A more hedonistic view of good and evil equates those states with pleasure and pain. Pleasure is good. Pain is evil. Therefore, one must spend their life in pursuit of what brings pleasure. This, of course, can create problems. If what causes me pleasure by its very nature requires someone else to suffer, am I doing good or evil?"

She pauses, and I shift in my chair, trying to wrap my mind around it all. "Should motives matter?" I ask. "If the motive is pure, does that justify evil deeds? If a few must be sacrificed for many more to live, is that evil or good?"

"I cannot say." Matilda leans forward, stoking the fire. "The balance of our acts and our intentions must be weighed by something far wiser than myself. I just know I have lived a very long life, and it will be longer still, and what I have seen of all creatures, human and otherwise, is that there will never be a consensus on what is truly right or wrong, good or evil. For that would require all species of beings to agree on what the primary objective of life is. Is it to be happy? To live well? To leave the world better than you found it? And what does that look like? Better for whom? Who decides what happiness means? What does 'better' even mean? And so, we must all muddle along, my dear. We must all make the best choices we can with the information we have about ourselves and the world, and self-correct along the way. Perhaps, the whole point of it all isn't to be good or even happy, but to continue learning. Perhaps, we are here to evolve, nothing more or less."

"There is darkness in me," I say. "I can see it now. I can feel it. And it makes me want to do things I used to believe were wrong. It makes me want to punish people who cause others harm. My brain says I should follow the appropriate paths for justice. Work within the system. But I know the system—all systems everywhere—are inherently corrupt. I know true justice—whatever that even is —will never really be accomplished. But if we all start enacting our own brand of justice based on our personal moral compasses, chaos will ensue. However, if we keep working within a corrupt system without challenging it, complacency will ensue and those who are disadvantaged by the system will always be so. I don't know the right answer."

She reaches over and takes my hand in hers. "And you may never know. There may not be 'the right answer' as you say, only what is the best choice in any given moment, which may not be the best choice in the next moment." She searches my face and smiles. "Find your balance. Do not let any one element within you become too dominate against the others, and you will find your way."

I look at my cup and realize it's empty. I yawn and stand. "Thank you."

She nods, staring into the fire. "He is in pain," she says after a moment.

"Who?" I ask.

"Cole. He is in pain. He will hurt others in his pain, but there is love in him, too." She looks up at me and smiles. "You can trust his love."

With a lightness of heart after talking to Matilda, I rejoin Cole in bed, curling my body into his, trusting his love. And knowing that life inherently holds pain, so we must hold onto to the joy when we have it.

OVER THE NEXT WEEK, we discuss the various ways to mount a proper defense for Liam. The ball was a bust and did not yield an egg or any leads. The Beggar Queen raised more questions than answers. And time is running out, as Derek keeps reminding us.

"I dug deeper into the basilisk guard who was found dead," Elijah says one morning over breakfast. "As I suspected, she had some skeletons in the closet. More specifically, skeletons in the dungeon. She has a brother serving hard time there."

"How would she have been allowed to work for Ava'Kara in such a sensitive position with a convicted criminal for a brother?" I ask, taking a bite of my egg on toast. "I would think the water dragon would do a thorough background check for anyone she let in her inner circle."

"She would have," Elijah says. "I had to use… controversial methods to discover this. And it wasn't easy."

I raise an eyebrow at that but don't press further. "We should pay this brother a visit, then," I say, glancing at Sebastian.

He nods. "Grab your cloak. We can go now."

On the way to the prison, Sebastian pulls out a leather-bound book and opens it. "Elijah made notes. Ethne Brinn's brother is named Lester Cornch. It looks like Ethne changed her last name to distance herself from her family. Their parents are deceased, as was previously indicated, but their deaths are a mystery. So is Lester's reason for conviction." He closes the notebook. "It's not much to go one, but maybe he can give us some ideas about who Ethne might have been working with and why."

I nod and lean back, closing my eyes. "We have to catch a break soon," I say softly, worried at what might happen to Liam, to this family, if we don't.

Sebastian takes my hand and squeezes it. "We will."

He's silent a moment, and when he speaks again, he sounds… unsure of himself, which is unusual for the earth Druid. "I noticed you have been spending a lot of time with Cole," he says.

I open my eyes and look at him. "Yes."

"This isn't about jealousy. I swear. We aren't like humans in that way. This is…just be careful, Eve. Cole is dangerous."

"Everyone in this world is dangerous," I remind him. "Including me."

"That's not what I mean. He's manipulative. Conniving. And I'm still not convinced his motives for being here are pure."

"I'll be careful," I promise him.

"That's all I ask. I…" he pauses. "I know I haven't been the most aggressive in pursuing you. Liam is all fire and passion and Cole…well, he's Cole. I've wanted to give you your space. Time to heal. Time to process all you've been through. But please know, Eve, that what I feel for you has been growing since the day we met on the subway. Since the moment I saw that portrait you drew of me."

His words make my heart beat faster and when he reaches over to caress my face, my stomach fills with butterflies. He leans over and kisses me tenderly, then pulls away. "I'm not going to push myself on you, but that doesn't me I don't want you. I want you more than I've ever wanted anything. But only when you're ready."

Dear god. I'm ready now, I want to tell him, but the carriage stops, and I realize we have arrived at the prison, so I just nod and smile and promise myself we will finish this conversation later.

We leave Lily—who is almost entirely healed—with the carriage and I follow Sebastian down a narrow cobblestone path. It's barely wide enough for one person to walk, and thorny bramble has taken over much of that room, leaving us both cut up and bleeding by the time we arrive at the massive building. Sebastian heals almost instantly, there are perks to being a vampire, it seems, but my cuts will take longer, of course.

The prison is a tall gothic cathedral made of black stone and sharp, spiky architecture. Atop it sits a massive black dragon, obsidian scales glimmering under the lights of the Dragon's Breath.

I can't tell if the dragon sees us or even cares that we're here. It seems to be content on its perch. "The Dragon of Darkness, I presume?" I ask Sebastian as we stop at the door. Beside the entrance are two skeletons, and it would have felt a bit Halloweenish except these are alive, and they scare the shit out of me when they step forward and demand to know what we want.

"We are here to see a prisoner in the course of an investigation," Sebastian says.

I flash my ring from Ava'Kara and Sebastian tells them who we want to see.

"Yes, that's the Dragon of Darkness," Sebastian says, as we follow one of the skeletons inside the building. "His name is Ra'Terr and he cares little for anything save guarding this prison. It's his magic that keeps so many creatures of different sizes, strengths, and abilities in check."

We step into a hallway lit only by torches set on the walls. It smells of brimstone and body odor and other—

worse—things. I try to breathe through my mouth, but then I can taste it, and that's even worse.

Sebastian smiles sympathetically at me.

"How can you stand it?" I ask.

"I can suspend my breathing when needed," he says, and I've never been more jealous of anyone.

The skeleton leads us down long stairways that feel as if they might crumble under my feet and down long halls lined with moaning and screaming prisoners of all species. There are no bars and when a man who looks like he's in mid transformation into a wolf lunges at us, I scream and unleash a fireball at him, only to realize that there's an invisible barrier that keeps him within his cage. He hits it —hard—and is zapped back to the other wall with a cry of pain. My fire hits the wall and fizzes to nothing.

We pass a mermaid a few cells farther down, her torso resting on a mat while her tail dangles in a small bucket of water. She looks close to death and I shudder to imagine what this must be like for her. But I also wonder what she did to deserve such a punishment. She glances at me with big coral eyes and a sadness so profound I want to weep just looking at her.

Finally, we step before a cell at the very end, and it's so dark within I can't tell who—or what—is inside. The skeleton taps on the invisible barrier. "You've got visitors."

He then leaves us alone, traveling with clacking bones back to his watch.

"I hope you were paying attention to how to get out of here," I say nervously. "It was a maze, and I didn't leave any breadcrumbs."

"I know my way around," Sebastian assures me.

A moment later, a slithering sound alerts us to the basilisk's presence. He comes close to the edge of the barrier, his forked tongue tasting the air around him. "What do you want, vampire?" he hisses.

Like Ethne, he is blindfolded. But unlike her, his seems permanently sewn into his face. Ouch.

"We came to ask you some questions about your sister," I say.

"I have no sssssisssster," he says.

"We know you do," Sebastian says. "And she's been killed. We're trying to find out what happened."

At the news that she's dead, the basilisk falls back, his tail faltering beneath him.

"Ethne is dead?"

"Yes," I say. "I'm sorry for your loss. Please help us figure out who did this and why."

He laughs, but it is a cold, hard, sad sound. "What would I know of anything, rotting in here for all eternity?"

"Ethne was a guard for Ava'Kara, and was killed while on duty," I say.

"Then you have the wrong persssssson," Lester says. "My sssssisssster—if I had one—would never work for the dragonsssss. Ssssshe'd die first."

Interesting. "And yet, she did. Work for them. And die," I say. "Don't you want to find out how? And why?"

When he says nothing, Sebastian continues. "It looks like she was involved in a plot to steal the water dragon's egg and was killed by her partner. Any idea who she might have been working with?"

Lester laughs again, and it sounds like the laugh of a madman. "That'sssss more like my Ethne. She has avenged our family at lasssst."

"What does that mean?" I ask. "Avenged your family for what?"

Lester lunges against the invisible wall, and when it zaps him, he doesn't even flinch. He presses his forehead against the force field, his face wild, the zaps crashing into him like lightning. "They did thissss to us, didn't they? They took it all. Everyone. Everything. Left ussss with nothing but liessss. All the liessss they bury here. This isn't a prisssson, it's a cemetery for enemiesss of the dragonsss. A grave for the barely living. She died in the fight against the lies. I live in the fight against the lies. The liessss eat ussss all."

"What do you mean?" I ask, leaning in. "What did the dragons do to your family?"

His tongue flicks out and he smiles widely. Too widely. "We knew their sssssecret, didn't we? The sssssecret they want hidden forever. The sssssecret of the world. The sssssecret to ssssaving it all. Their sssselfish, lying, evil sssssecret that fills this place with rot and shit and the carcasses of truth once sssspoken."

"What secret?" I ask.

"The sssssecret. The sssssecret. The ssssssecret." His voice escalates as he keeps repeating it, over and over.

"What secret!" I shout, trying to be heard over his insanity.

He slams his body so hard against the invisible shield that I can practically feel the zaps of electricity shooting through the wall and into him. My skin tingles with the magic around me, tapping into my own pools of power.

He flicks his tongue, licking at the invisible wall. Then he sniffs and smiles.

"You're the sssssecret. You're the ssssssecret. You're the

169

sssssecret." With a sudden movement, he slams his head into the shield so hard his skin splits open and he falls to the ground, writhing on the floor as the magic electrocutes him.

Sebastian pulls me away. "We have to go!"

I'm too shaken to argue with him, and it's clear we won't get any more answers from Lester, if we got anything at all.

Sebastian guides us through the maze of stairs and halls until we reach the front door.

Rather than head home, we take a detour and stop at a pub.

"You need food and we both need a drink," Sebastian says.

The Naked Gnome is indeed run by a gnome who likes to flaunt his nether regions at his place of business. Not the choice I would have made, but I shrug and go along with it.

"Ignore him," Sebastian says of the gnome who's presently dancing on the bar, doing his best free willy interpretation. "The food here is excellent."

I raise an eyebrow at that. "How would you know? You don't eat."

"I've been told," he says with a crooked grin.

"I hope his bits aren't part of the food prep process?"

Sebastian laughs. "No, he sticks to the bar. He likes the audience."

I look around at the empty pub. "Audience?"

Sebastian shrugs and when a very old and very small woman comes to take our order, I ask him to pick something he thinks I will like.

My mind is stuck on Lester's ranting. "What did he mean about a secret?" I ask.

"The dragons undoubtedly have many secrets," Sebastian says. "But what secret that could save the world? I have no idea."

"And what do I have to do with it?" I wonder. "Or was that just his insanity?"

"I would bet insanity, but we shouldn't rule anything out."

Drinks are brought to us, and I am served a plate of potatoes, meat, and a garden salad. "What kind of meat?" I ask suspiciously.

"Just eat the potatoes and salad," he says by way of answer. "We don't have cows in this world."

Yup, still a vegetarian, at least while we're in the Otherworld.

Under my plate is a recent copy of town news, and I scan the headlines until I see one that ruins my appetite and makes my blood run cold.

"What is it?" Sebastian asks.

I push the paper over to him. "Look."

Anger is clouding my judgment and when my fists turn to balls of fire, Sebastian pays quickly and escorts me out.

"How could this happen?" I ask.

"It's not a perfect system," Sebastian says.

I spin on him. "Not perfect? Not perfect? We're not even in the ballpark of perfect. We're so far from perfect right now that even adequate is out of reach. Competence is a laughable dream. This is a disgrace. This is evil!"

Lily pulls the carriage up and raises an eyebrow when she sees me. "What happened?"

Sebastian answers for me since I'm still too rage-monster to speak in coherent sentences. "The Collector was released from prison. He won't face charges."

Lily flinches as if physically punched, then shakes her head sadly.

Before we take off, I make a decision. "Lily, take us by Lilith's house on the way home. I need to call in a favor."

THE PARTY

There is nothing more important than love. And no law higher.
~Lady Midnight by Cassandra Clare

MY VISIT with Lilith yields the results I expect, but I'm still struggling with my decision. Am I stepping over the line? Sliding down a slippery slope? I believe what I've done is the right choice. The just choice.

It's just not the legal choice.

Now I wait to hear back from her.

I also have a shit ton of work to do.

For two weeks, time passes at breakneck speed. We leave no stone unturned in trying to suss out the ravings of a madman, and we make no progress in figuring out what the dragons might be lying about. We already knew Ethne had no love lost for the dragons, if she was willing to betray Ava'Kara and steal her egg, so the news that their family bore a grudge against the dragons doesn't help our case any. Not unless we could figure out why, and not unless that why is connected to her motive and could also connect us to her partner/killer.

All in all, it's a waste. Our strongest argument is lack of evidence on the part of the prosecutor, but given that's Dath'Racul himself, I doubt very much that will be enough to get Liam a Not Guilty verdict.

"How can they let him prosecute?" I ask, for probably the millionth time since I found out. "He's got way too much power to make a fair prosecutor."

"It's not fair," Liam says, fire sparking at the tips of his fingers. "But nothing about this system is fair."

The other three brothers agree. Cole is the only one missing. He never attends meetings about Liam's court case, arguing he's not a lawyer and has done all he can to help. He's likely at the local pub enjoying a strong drink. I could use a strong drink myself at this point.

Matilda comes in carrying a tray of goblets and food. "You lot have been at this long enough. Have you not noticed the date?"

Elijah's eyes widen. "It's New Year's Eve tomorrow. And the court case is the next day."

Liam frowns. "There's nothing more we can do. Justice will prevail or it won't. This might be my last holiday with those I love the most," he says, his gaze locking on mine. "And I want to celebrate it. Put the law books away. And let's prepare the castle for a proper New Year's celebration."

Derek stops his pacing, hands locked behind his back, and glances at Liam. "We can't give up."

"It's not giving up," Liam says. "It's recognizing we are as prepared as we possibly can be. At the end of the day, they have no evidence against me. That's going to have to be enough. It's not our job to prove who the real criminal is. It's their job to prove it's me. And they can't." He shrugs, and as hot tempered as the fire Druid can be, he seems to be learning when to let things go.

Now is one of those times. I can see it in him. He needs to have a family celebration. Some joy. Some time with his daughter.

"I agree with Liam," I say. "This time of year is about family. Let's make happy memories while we can."

Matilda smiles gently at me, and the others finally stop arguing and stop working and we break to begin preparations for the party.

Lily sends out beautifully calligraphed invitations to our closest friends, while I work with the castle ghosts to discuss the decorations. Well, discuss might be stretching that word's definition a bit. More like, I talk to an empty room and hope someone is listening.

I have no idea if this is a gift-giving event, but I have a surprise for the family, and as I spend a few hours alone in my room, I put the polishing touches on it, admiring the finished results. A door opens and I spin around and come face to face with Cole, who stands transfixed by the painting I've been working on for weeks.

It's a watercolor painting of all of us, the five Night brothers, Matilda, Lily, me, Alina, and of course, Moon, who is presently curling around my ankles begging to be pet.

"You painted this?" Cole asks, stepping forward to study it.

"Yes."

"It should be in a museum."

I feel heat rise to my cheeks. "Thank you. I'm quite proud of it."

He smiles, redirecting his gaze to me. "You should be."

Cole cups my face and leans in to kiss me, his breath mixing with mine, his lips like velvet, and I melt into him as I feel his shadow magic wrap around me, caressing me everywhere at once.

He pulls away just enough to speak, his dark eyes so penetrating. "Leave with me," he says in a breath, and I freeze and step back.

"What?"

"Leave with me. Just you and me. We can start a new life anywhere in any world we want." He looks so earnest. So desperate for me to say yes.

"This is my home," I say. "My family. Your family."

He scoffs. "I don't belong here. I'm an outcast to my brothers. And an outsider in this world. But with you, I can be anything. Do anything. You and I are so much stronger together than apart. Can't you feel it?"

The thing is, I can. I can feel how my magic responds to Cole when he is close to me. How the power within me swells and rises, as if being summoned and magnified. It's a heady feeling, and I want to cling to it. To him. But…to leave? Just like that?

And then I remember my brother's words.

That I will be given the chance to leave, and I must take it. I must leave the Night brothers.

Is this what he meant? Is this the moment that will define my life?

I haven't seen or heard from my brother since he gave me this ring. I fidget with it as I consider my choices. If my brother truly is seeing the future, then I should leave with Cole. I should start a life with him. And it would be an amazing life, I do believe that. But it would mean saying goodbye to Liam, to Liam's daughter who has become like my own, to Sebastian, and Derek, and Elijah, all of whom I have growing feelings towards. To Matilda and Lily. The Ifrits. All of my friends here.

I haven't had time to give it much thought, but I've just realized how much I have here. How many roots I've put down. How many people I would miss, beyond just the men I'm falling in love with.

This is the moment I must decide if I truly believe my brother's visions.

If I leave with Cole, then it means I believe what my brother did by killing Mary and the baby truly will have saved many lives.

If I stay...does that mean I am saying I don't believe my brother? Which means he wasn't justified in killing them, and that makes him...evil? Or insane, but then very dangerous.

How can I decide this, right here, right now? How can I possibly have enough knowledge and wisdom to weigh those possibilities?

"Eve?" Cole's voice is broken.

And it breaks me.

Tears stream down my face. "Stay. Just stay. Let us all be a family. Your niece needs you. And whether they know it or not, your brothers need you."

I step forward and wrap my arms around his waist. "I need you."

"You don't know what you're asking," he says. "You don't know who I really am."

"Then stay and show me," I say. "Or stay and change.

177

Each moment we get a chance to redeem ourselves. To reimagine who we choose to be. Use this moment now. Whatever is in your heart, whatever pain, whatever anger, whatever demons, let it go. And stay."

He kisses me and smiles. "You're truly a remarkable woman, Eve. I didn't expect you in my life."

And then he leaves, and I realize he never did promise he'll stay. I can only hope my words take root within him. This family needs to heal. And none of them can do that if Cole leaves.

* * *

THE NEXT DAY there is a flurry of activity as we all ready for the party. Elijah comes to my room with a long silver box. I open it and find a gorgeous red velvet dress perfectly sized for me. "Wow! Thank you."

"It compliments your complexion," he says, and then kisses my cheek and leaves quickly, as if slightly embarrassed.

Lily comes to my aid, helping me dress and style my hair. I study myself in the mirror and twirl around, smiling. It's a melancholic smile, with the looming threat of trial the next day, but I'm determined to enjoy the time we have tonight, with dear friends and family.

I wonder if Adam will show up again, or if I've seen my brother for the last time. I have no way of contacting him. No way of getting a message to him. No way of knowing if he's dead or alive. Can he even die? I have no way of knowing that, either.

Lily curls my hair and folds it into an updo, with soft

ringlets let down around my face, and red holly tucked into the braid.

I stain my lips red and line my eyes with kohl, and then Lily and I walk down, arm and arm. She's dressed in green, and together we look quite festive.

I'm relieved to see Cole by the front door with his brothers as they greet guests.

Ifi and Elal arrive first, and the two Ifrits greet us quickly then make a beeline straight to the baby. Matilda hands her over and the two of them nearly set the house on fire with their excitement. I'm about to warn them to be careful with Alina, when she throws a fireball and one of them catches it and tosses it back to her.

Liam laughs and Matilda clucks her tongue. "We really need to come up with a spell to ward off fire damage, with all you fire elements running around." She looks meaningfully at Liam and me, and the Ifrits both raise their eyebrows. Ifi thrusts his hip out and shakes his finger at me. "Girl, you are holding out. You got fire power now?"

I laugh and hold up my palm, producing a single, perfect flame in it. Then I aim at the candles lining the mantle over the fireplace and light all five of them at once. Not a single one melts on contact.

Liam claps, a huge smile on his face. "You've been practicing."

I nod. "Yes."

A knock on the door draws everyone's attention and Kana the Kitsune enters in her beautiful woman form. Her long, glossy black hair flows unbridled down the back of her floor-length, silver evening gown. As soon as she sees me, she checks that I'm wearing the amulet she gave me, and nods when she sees the crystal pendant with the fox carved into its face hanging at my collarbone.

Elijah offers his elbow and escorts her into the ballroom where we've set up tables of food and drink. It turns out the ghosts of the castle included some musicians, so we enjoy a haunted concert, as a cello, piano, bass, viola, and violin all begin to play as if on their own.

Akuro and Okura arrive next with their bundle of joy, and the Ifrits squeal in delight at another baby. The two couples head into the ballroom with the babies to let them play together.

Lily hasn't joined in the festivities and I notice she keeps glancing at the door. I find out why a few minutes later when Kaya arrives, wearing a gold dress that compliments Lily's. They both smile beatifically when they see each other, and they move into the corner to talk, holding hands the whole time.

I'm grinning from ear to ear like an idiot when Liam walks over to me and slips his arm around my waist. "You look happy, love," he says, kissing my cheek.

"I like seeing Lily happy," I say, nodding to her and Kaya.

Liam raises an eyebrow. "She does indeed look happy." He smiles. "Good for her."

He turns back to me, his face becoming more serious. "Can I talk to you? Alone?"

"Sure," I say, following him out of the ballroom and into the library. "What's up?"

He closes the door behind us and pulls out a parchment, handing it to me. "I want you to have this, in case... well, just in case."

My stomach drops as I realize what he's doing, and I

squeeze the parchment in my fist, resisting the urge to give it back to him. Tears sting my eyes. "We are going to win. You're going to be fine."

"Maybe," he says. "But, maybe not. There's a strong chance I don't come out of this well. If that happens, I need to ask you the biggest favor I've ever asked anyone."

I try to swallow, but my mouth and throat have suddenly dried out. "What?"

"Take care of Alina. Adopt her. Be her mother. If I know she has you, I can face whatever is coming."

Now the tears flow, and I pull Liam into a hug, clinging to him as if the fierceness of my love is enough to save him. "You know I'll always take care of that little girl," I say. "Always."

Liam pulls back to study me. "Even if I'm found innocent, I'd...I'd still like you to adopt her. To officially become her mother, if you're willing. You're the only mother she has."

I can't speak. My heart is flooding with emotion, my body viscerally moved by his trust in me, by this shared bond that is so heavy and yet so light all at the same time. "Are you sure that's what you want?" I ask.

He nods. "More than anything. I want you and I want her. The two of you are my family."

He kisses me deeply and it feels as if it might be the last time we ever kiss like this again, though I know that's not possible. We have time before the trial. Time to steal more kisses and hold each other and talk about the future with his daughter. Our daughter.

It's a perfect moment.

Until it isn't.

A warning flash hits me first, sending a wave of dizziness through me.

Then a loud crash coming from the hall startles us both into action. When Liam and I run out, we see the front door has been beaten down and Enforcers swarm into the castle led by Dath'Racul. He tips his head at me, "Miss Oliver." His eyes narrow when he sees Liam.

"We have a warrant to search this property." He hands Liam a scroll, and Liam studies it, singeing the edges with his fire.

I read over his shoulder and my blood runs cold.

They had a tip. The egg is somewhere in the castle, and once they find it, any defense we might have had falls apart.

THE LIE

How does something that set fire to your heart suddenly chill your bones? ~Nikita Gill

ENFORCERS IMMEDIATELY BEGIN to spread out, roughly handling priceless antiques as they search in the most unlikely places.

"The egg, which is the size of a medium built dog, is not hiding in a vase the size of my first," I say, grabbing the ancient hand-painted relic from an Enforcer's hand. "Are you here to destroy everything, or to actually attempt to find a dragon egg?" I ask.

Matilda, Lily, the other brothers, the Ifrits, the Kitsune, the Gargoyles and the Dryad all come to the hall after hearing the commotion. The baby is crying and the Enforcers look at each other, uncomfortable with the presence of a child, clearly.

Derek steps forward, frowning. "What's the meaning of this, Racul? You know we don't have the egg."

The fire dragon shrugs. "Then you shouldn't have any problem with us taking a look around."

My flash is still pinging in my brain, but I don't need my flash to know something smells off about this whole thing. I grab Derek's hand and pull him into another room while the others continue asking questions and generally work to keep the Enforcers from making much progress in their search.

"This is a set up," I tell Derek in a whisper. Who knows what kinds of creatures the Enforcers are, or how well they can hear.

"I assume so as well."

"Which means, the egg is here. Someone is framing Liam. We have to find the egg and get rid of it before they do, or there's nothing we'll be able to say to exonerate Liam."

Derek nods.

"You know the castle better than me. It will be somewhere that looks like it's been hidden, but not so hidden that these idiots won't find it," I say.

"The Enforcers may be idiots, but don't underestimate Dath'Racul. He's shrewd and brilliant."

I narrow my eyes. "So am I."

Derek smiles at that. "That you are."

We head to my room where I get my sketchbook and turn to the pages I drew when I first arrived here, of all the halls and rooms and secret passages I could find in the castle. Derek whistles under his breath. "I'm not sure you're assessment is correct," he says.

"About what?"

"I don't think I know this castle better than you. That's the most thorough map I've ever seen."

"Let's hit up all the bedrooms as fast as we can, then head to the more remote areas."

We work quickly searching through each room—my god there are so many—and tracking our progress on my drawing. We search Liam's room more thoroughly since that would be an extra nail in the coffin if it's found in there. But…nothing.

We then head down to the lower levels, to where Lily's tree lives, to places that used to be prisons and give me the chills to be in. Moon follows at our heels, as if he understands what we're doing and wants to help.

We can hear the Enforcers hitting the places as we leave them.

When our search yields nothing, I sigh, then have a light bulb moment and grab Derek's hand. "I think I know where it is."

We've been to all the main levels, and we've been below. The only place we haven't checked is up. The stairway that winds up the tallest tower is dark and narrow, and the higher we go, the less covering we have from the storm that's brewing. Wind and rain pelt us as we reach the top platform. At first it appears we've reached another dead end, but then, in the corner, I see a trunk that wasn't here before. I show Derek, who walks over and tries to open it. "It's locked."

Derek is water, and that's not going to help us right now. "Stand back," I say, praying I have enough control for this. Because if the egg is in there, and I mess up, well, I can't think too much about that without having a panic attack.

I definitely do not want to kill a baby dragon. That's for sure not on my list of things to ever do.

I pull up the fire in me and direct it into the metal lock, heating it up until it's so hot it cracks, falling off. Derek reaches for it, but I hold him back. "You'll burn yourself."

Instead, I grab it and pull it open, knowing I am now immune to fire. My powers are growing.

And just as I suspected. Within the chest is the pulsing silver blue egg of the water dragon. I can feel the life growing within, and I lay a hand on it and close my eyes, letting the feeling of bliss from this little being wash over me.

A zapping sound startles me and Derek yelps and falls to the ground. I spin around, stunned to see Derek unconscious. I run to him and hold his head in my lap, trying to revive him. I'm about to slit my wrists to feed him when a voice stops me.

"Eve, leave him. He is not badly injured. He will wake and be fine."

I look up at Adam and frown. "What are you doing here? Why did you attack Derek?"

Laying Derek gently on the ground, I stand, facing my twin. "What's going on, Adam? Did you steal the dragon egg?"

"I had to," he says, with the same conviction he used to defend his murder of Mary and her child. "This is all happening the way it needs to. The Enforcers must find the egg. Liam must take the fall. If he doesn't…"

"What? What happens if Liam isn't blamed for a crime he didn't commit?" I ask, my patience for all this nonsense wearing thin.

"You die," he says. "You, the baby, all the other brothers, Matilda, Lily and her tree…you all die. You burn to death."

I shake my head. "That's impossible. I have the fire element in me. So does Alina. She and I can't burn to death."

He shrugs. "I've seen it, Evie. It happens. Or it would have, if I hadn't intervened. Whatever leads up to it, somehow this particular fire destroys you all. And when Liam discovers what he's done, he takes his own life. This way is better, for him and for all of you. You must let it happen."

"You want me to believe that we should play god with people's lives based on visions of a future that may or may not happen?" I ask. "I can't do that. It isn't right."

"You have always been so caught up with doing the right thing, you've never stopped to ask yourself where this idea of right and wrong even came from. Or if it even makes sense." He runs a hand through his hair and sighs. "Isn't it a greater good to save many, even if it means sacrificing a few?"

I shake my head, stepping back. "This doesn't feel right."

"Come with me, Evie. Let's leave. Together. Just you and me. Us against the world, like it always used to be." He holds out his hand, his eyes pleading. "I can't do this without you. We are stronger together. We always have been."

My heart stops. When it beats again, it fills my head with the sound. Everything slows. My breathing hitches. And then...everything falls into place and I swallow a bitter truth that cracks me open and leaves me shredded.

Adam has been pushing me to leave the Night Firm.

He showed me the Memory Catcher, which he knew would create conflict with Liam and the other brothers.

The demon the Collector subjected me to said, "Nothing is at it appears. Least of all fate's twins."

And the other night at the ball, Cole used shadow magic to change his features.

I want to deny the truth I feel in my own soul, but I can't.

"You're not Adam, are you…. Cole?"

Adam sighs and a black mist floats over him. When it clears, Cole stands in his place. "I'm impressed you figured it out. Most people only see what they want to see."

"I never wanted to see my brother turn into murderer," I say, spitting out the words. "How could you lie to me like that, then sleep with me?"

"I never wanted to hurt you," he says. "You are collateral damage in a much larger war."

"That's all I am? Collateral damage? All in an effort to punish your brothers? To punish Liam?" I feel crushed inside, but I can't give into my despair just yet. There's still the egg, and the Enforcers. "Don't you understand that Liam's been punishing himself for years? He's the one who wanted to make amends. He's a father now. He has a little girl who needs him."

Cole's face twists into an ugly smile. "They will be here at any moment," he says. "They'll arrest Liam. Hell, they'll probably arrest all of my brothers. You should leave with me now, Eve, so you don't get caught up in this mess. I still mean what I said. I need you. We are stronger together."

"The memory you showed me… did you kill Mary and the baby looking like my brother?" My only comfort in this moment is that my brother is still the man I carry in my memories. The man who couldn't hurt a fly, who was too gentle and kind for his own good. Cole nearly took that away from me.

"No," he says. "I didn't kill them. That memory was fake, created by shadow magic." He steps forward. "You could do so much with your power, Eve. I can show you. You have no idea what you're capable of with all the elements in you."

I still feel drawn to him, despite everything that he's done, and it kills me to pull away, to deny my feelings, to go against this pull that has entranced me since I first saw him at the festival.

"How did you know how to be Adam so perfectly?"

"Your dreams," Cole says. "He lives in your dreams and I can dream walk."

"What about the guard? The basilisk?" I ask. "You killed her. She was your partner and you killed her."

He shakes his head. "No. Ethne was supposed to live. She injured herself to look innocent and was meant to keep her cover. My guess is one of the dragons killed her for failing to protect the egg."

"How do I know you're telling me the truth?" I ask.

"Look at your ring," he says.

Confused, I look at my finger. The onyx is glowing, and it occurs to me Adam didn't give me this. Cole did.

Shit.

I'm going to have to go back and re-remember every damn conversation I had with who I thought was my brother and replace that face with Cole's.

"That ring has a part of me—a part of my magic—in it. And a part of you," he says. "You can use it to tell if someone lies to you."

"How?" I ask.

He cocks his head. "Eve, I hate you."

His words are a punch to the gut, but when I look down at the ring, it's pulsing.

"Eve," he says, softly. "I love you."

The ring goes back to glowing.

"That's how," he says.

And my heart is ripped into pieces once again.

"Cole?" Derek's voice is hallow and weak, and I turn to see him sitting up. "It was you this whole time?" A tear slides down Derek's face. "We deserve this. But I deserve it the most. I may not have been the one to land the whip on you, but...I'm the one who turned you in after I found out what you did. If it weren't for me, none of this would be happening. If you must punish anyone, take me. Leave the rest of them out of it. Please. I'm so sorry, brother."

Cole scowls. "You will need to pay for that," he says. "But that doesn't exonerate the rest of them. You all played your part in my torture and imprisonment. And you will all suffer the consequences of your actions. You believe in justice? This is justice."

A black swirl appears around Cole, and I can tell he's about use his shadow powers to escape. I can't let him.

I plunge into my powers and break the wall I'd been keeping around my darkness, dipping into the inky magic that lives in my deepest depths, and I pull it up, letting it wrap around me, then I use a strand of it to tug at Cole.

Just as he's about to vanish, leaving his brothers stranded with the incriminating egg, I latch onto him and his smoke dissipates. He looks at me, wide eyed. "How did you do that?"

"I finally realized you're right. I'm more powerful

when I tap into my darkness. But it has to be on my terms, even if I don't totally know what those terms are."

With my powers fully open, I feel my veins fill with all the elements, and I tremble from the influx of magic surging within me. My body rises from the ground, hovering, my arms spread, my skin glowing as the storm around us rages.

And suddenly my mind is flooded with a history of memories that don't belong to me, but I see it all, in an instant, the past and present and future are one, and my thoughts expand beyond what I thought possible.

When I open my mouth to speak, it is not my words that come forth, and it is not my voice that is heard.

"If you are going to punish anyone, Son of Light, punish me," the being within me says through my mouth. "It is not your brothers who are to blame, but myself. I was the one who decided on your punishment. I was the one who condemned you for what I thought I saw." I flick my wrist and summon a whip made of golden light, it's edge rzor sharp. "If you must inflict pain on your tormenter, then whip me. Punish me." I hold out the whip, unafraid of what is to come. I accept whatever choice is made. "Or, you can break the cycle of pain and punishment and revenge. You can change the karmic path of everyone in this house and you can forgive, as I should have forgiven you. As I now do. You are forgiven, Son of Light, and restored with full honor and apologies to the Order of the Druids, should you wish to return. I cannot take away what is done, but I can offer this." With another flick of my wrist, a glowing golden light travels from my fingertips to Cole, and runs over his body. His eyes widen and he lifts his shirt, marveling as the scars from his torture disappear, replaced by healthy skin.

The magic still buzzes through me, and I see what happened to him all those years ago. The blood and tears and pain. The humiliation. The betrayal. And as much as I feel hurt and betrayed by a man I love, I also see the pain that led him down this path. And I know that whatever voice is speaking through me, I also need to follow heed and forgive, as hard as it is.

Cole leans forward, and I close my eyes, resigned as he reaches for the whip.

I will accept the lashes. The punishment.

I will accept whatever karmic end I must.

But when nothing happens, I open my eyes. The whip is still in my hand. But the egg—and Cole—are both gone.

THE GOODBYE

Girls like her were born in a storm. They have lightning in their souls, thunder in their hearts, and chaos in their bones.
~Nikita Gill

WITH MY POWER DRAINED, I fall to my knees, bruising them on the stone floor. Derek's strong arms pull me towards him and keep me from hitting the ground face first. I feel as if my power, my energy, has been sucked dry. In a panic, I dive into myself, to my core, and to my relief I still see a small trickle of each element within me.

"My magic," I whisper, my eyes fluttering closed as darkness pulls at my consciousness. "It's almost gone."

Derek kisses my forehead. "You're okay. Just rest."

* * *

I WAKE in the way one does when they don't know how

much time has passed or what day it is and there was something very important to do.

"The trial!" I yell, startling Liam, who is dozing in the chair next to my bed.

He rubs his eyes, then smiles when he sees I've returned to the land of the living. "You gave us a scare," he says, coming to sit on the bed next to me.

He hands me a glass of water and I down the entire thing in one gulp. He refills from a pitcher on my side table, and I drink that as well. Three cups later and I feel like a water balloon about ready to burst, but the cobwebs are finally clearing out of my head.

He hands me one more cup, and I'm about to decline, but I sniff it and realize it's not water. "Matilda?" I ask.

He smiles and nods. "You won't like it, but it will help you get your strength, and magic, back sooner."

It's worth it, I suppose. I gag it down and try not to vomit, then look around for some indication of what time it is.

"We need to get to the trial." I say, putting the cup down and trying to crawl out of bed, but Liam stills me with a hand on my knee.

"There was no trial," he says grinning.

"What? Why?"

"Charges against me have been dropped. Lack of evidence, I guess." He shrugs. "I'm free."

It takes a moment for his words to sink in, and when they do, my heart nearly bursts from the joy of it. I reach for him, sliding one hand behind his head, letting my fingers dig into his hair, as I pull his face towards mine. Our lips brush against each other gently at first, then he groans and scoots our hips closer, deepening our kiss as he does.

Just as our passions rise, Liam pauses, resting his lips against my neck as he holds me close. "You're still recovering. The healer in me can't let this go further until you have all your strength back."

I sigh and kiss his neck, to let him know what I think of his restraint. He groans again. "You're killing me, Eve."

Within his arms, while enjoying the scent of him and feel of him, I dive into myself again and am relieved to discover the elements within me are growing once more. I didn't lose my magic, it was just tapped out. Good to know that can happen.

And then my thoughts return to the trial, and I sit back. "I don't understand. Even without evidence, it seemed the dragons were determined to use you as the fall guy for this. What changed?"

"I don't know. But I'm grateful."

I smile. "So am I. Now Alina won't have to grow up without her father."

He nods. "What we talked about before…"

"It's okay if you want to change your mind about me adopting her," I say, though in my heart I had come to want it very badly. But still, I can't hold him to something he decided when he thought he was going away for life, or worse.

"I'm not changing my mind, Eve," he says, shaking his head as if I'm being absurd. "I'm checking to see if you've changed yours. I would understand, though I hope you haven't."

"I haven't," I say. "I want to be her mother. More than anything."

He smiles with true abandon, and it warms my heart, but then a sinking sensation steals over me. "But first, I need to tell you something, and it may affect your decision about this."

"I doubt it," he says. "But go ahead."

And so, I tell him everything. About Adam—or who I thought was Adam. About lying to him and about what came out of me when my powers activated during my confrontation with Cole.

"The weird thing was, when my powers hit, I was me but not me. Like someone else was speaking through me. I don't know how to explain it, but I said things that didn't make sense." I pause, frowning. "Anyways, I thought you should know all that before deciding on something so important. I know you're probably furious with me, and I don't blame you."

I wait for him to explode, to rage, to...I don't know, lose his temper, but instead he blinks.

That's it.

Just a blink.

"I've been wondering when you would tell me about Adam," he says, shocking the living hell out of me. "I've known for a while. I overheard the two of you at the Midwinter Festival. Though I must say, I'm so sorry my brother deceived you like that. That was cruel, even for him."

My heart lurches, both in relief that Liam isn't as angry as I thought he would be, and in renewed grief at remembering my brother really is still dead, and always was. Thinking I had him back, even knowing what he had become, gave me comfort. I didn't feel so alone in the world, knowing he was still in it.

He was the last person left alive who knew me as a child, who shared those memories of us growing up. Now, they live in me alone.

"Why didn't you say something if you already knew?" I ask.

"Why didn't you tell me?" he replies.

"Well, you are known for having quite the temper," I say. "And I didn't know what to do about Adam. He's my twin. I had to sort out what the right course of action was, and I didn't want you killing him."

A knock at the door interrupts us, and Matilda comes in. "I thought you might be awake," she says, smiling. "You have a visitor, my dear. Lilith is here for you."

"Thank you. I need a few minutes to freshen up. Can you tell her I'll be down shortly?"

Matilda nods and leaves, and Liam stands. "Do you want assistance dressing?" he asks.

I laugh. "I thought we weren't supposed to fool around? Doctor's orders or something?"

"There will be no fooling around. Strictly platonic."

He holds up his hands innocently, then slips one arm around me to help me from the bed. My legs are wobbly, and I walk about as well as a newborn colt. "How long will I feel this way?" I ask.

"It will take time for your strength and powers to return," he says as he guides me to the bathroom. "But I don't know specifically. You're a bit of an anomaly in the magical world, as I'm sure you've realized."

With Liam's totally platonic (sadly) help, I manage to bathe, brush my hair and teeth, and change into something appropriate. While dressing I notice the ring Cole gave me is missing from my finger. "Did you see my ring?" I ask. "Silver with black onyx."

"I know the one you're talking about, but no. I haven't seen it," Liam says.

Huh. It must have fallen off when my powers went all supernova.

I feel a sinking loss at that, at this one little piece I had of Cole. Despite my feelings for him being complicated, I can't change the bond we have. I can't pretend it doesn't exist, even within my hurt and anger.

Because when I think back to what he's gone through. From early childhood abuse into the adulthood that removed him from his life and family, I can see how he ended up where he did. Who's to say any of us would have acted any differently in the same circumstances.

Liam helps me downstairs and Matilda has food and wine waiting in the sitting room for me, and blood for Lilith, of course. I'm surprised to see she's brought someone with her. The cat girl from the Collector's party.

Lilith stands when I enter, then rushes to help me get seated. "What happened to you?" she asks. "You're as pale as...well, me."

"It's a long story," I say, taking a plate of food.

I glance at the girl and smile. "You look well... er, I realize I don't know your name. I'm Eve."

She nods. "I'm Sasha. Thank you. For...everything. Lilith told me what you did for me."

I direct a questioning look to Lilith, who shrugs. "She didn't have anywhere to go, so I took her in. I figured I could use a protégé. I have many businesses in this world and the mundane and no heirs. This seemed a perfect fit for us both."

I grin and offer the girl a plate of fresh bread and berries, which she accepts.

"That makes me incredibly happy," I say. "And the other matter?"

"Yes, the favor you asked of me," Lilith says with a devious smile. "It's been handled. The Collector has found himself indisposed for the foreseeable future."

"And there's no chance of him escaping or being found?" I ask. I may have crossed a line, asking Lilith to find a place the Collector could serve the prison sentence he deserves. But isn't this justice? Letting him go free to enslave and hurt others wouldn't have served anyone.

I've realized about myself two things since all that's happened with Cole and with who I thought was Adam. One: I've got a lot more darkness in me than I wanted to admit. And two: it's okay. I can use that darkness. I don't have to stay within the lines to feel morally comfortable with my decisions, but I can't act out of vengeance and I can't kill unless I'm actively defending myself or someone else. My choices have to be just, even if they aren't always lawful.

It's an ambitious line that not all would agree with, but it's what feels right to me, at least for now.

"He will never be found or escape, of that you have my word," Lilith says. "Would you like me to take you to him so you can see for yourself?"

"No, though I appreciate the offer. I actually have something else I need to deal with right now. And I trust you."

Lilith stands. "Very well then, I must be off. But stay in touch, Eve. I truly enjoy our friendship, and despite having lived longer than almost anyone, I can't actually call many people 'friend.'"

Her words touch me. Deeply. I stand and hug her. "I value this as well," I say. "And I'll pay a visit soon. Once the dust settles with all this stolen egg business."

Lilith's eyes widen and she reaches into her bag. "That reminds me. I was asked to deliver this to you."

She hands me a scroll, sealed with a dragon mark. I break the wax and read. "It's from Ava'Kara. She wants to meet with me later today. Alone." I look up at Lilith. "Do you know what this is about?"

"I haven't got a clue," she says, "but I wouldn't be late if I were you."

Once they leave, I head to my room and stand before the mantle, staring at my brother's urn. Funny that I never got rid of it once I thought he was alive. Maybe a part of me always knew it wasn't really Adam visiting me. But like Cole said, we see what we want to. I wanted to believe Adam was alive. I wanted to believe I hadn't lost my brother forever.

I take the urn and walk outside. Moon follows close behind. Sebastian notices me leaving but sees what I'm holding and doesn't interfere.

My strength is returning to me faster than I expected. The potion must have helped. I feel strong enough to make the walk I need to. Beyond our property, just past a grove of trees, is the shoreline for the only ocean on this world. I saw it on a map and have been wanting to visit but haven't had time.

Today I'm making time.

Today I'm going to finally say goodbye to my brother.

With Moon the only witness, I stand on the shore,

overlooking the horizon, where the deep purples of the Dragon's Breath dance over the waters that ebb and flow. I take off my shoes and let my toes sink into the wet sand, the salty water covering them with each tide.

As tears flow down my cheek, I taste the salt of them on my lips, I realize we are all made of the ocean. Salt and water and tides and depth and mystery and wonder. And so, I return my brother to the watery arms of the sea, to be held by her.

I open the urn and tilt it, but the air is stagnate and doesn't catch the ashes.

Closing my eyes, I dip into my power and pull just enough from air to encourage a breeze that takes my brother's remains and sweeps them into the water.

"Goodbye, Adam," I whisper, letting the wind carry my words with his body. "Every day I think of you. Every day I wish things had gone differently for us. You should be here with me, exploring this new world, enjoying this new family. They would love you. You'd have brothers. So many brothers." I chuckle. As children, I used to dress up like a boy and pretend to be Adam's brother sometimes, so the other boys wouldn't refuse to play with us.

"I wish I could go back in time, to the day before you died, and tell you all that is in my heart. Tell you that I would have endured a thousand bankruptcies and shitty apartments to have you back. I wish I could tell you how much I love you. How much I miss you. How a piece of me died with you."

I choke on my words as the urn empties, and I watch as his ashes drift on the current.

"I wish I could tell you there were other options. Other choices. You didn't have to take your life."

I wipe my eyes and think back on all the beautiful memories we shared as children. Even the hardest times feel sweet in reflection, because I had him. "I hope more than anything that you have found peace. That whatever awaits us in the afterlife has brought you healing and joy. Someday we will be together again. Until then and always, I will carry you in my heart."

THE SACRIFICE

Your love was born in the wild, growing from the soft earth surrounded by trees that were surrounded by stars. That is why the forest has such a hold on you. That is why sometimes if feels like the moon knows your name.

~Your Love by Nikita Gill

"I'll be with her," Lily argues, setting her glass of berry juice down firmly.

Sebastian crosses his arms over his chest, for the millionth time, and huffs.

I'm sick and tired of this argument. "This isn't a discussion," I say. "The note said to come alone. I'm not even sure Lily should be there."

Now it's Lily's turn to huff. "Of course, I should be there. Who else will drive you? Do you know how to effectively guide a horse drawn carriage?" she asks pointedly.

My mouth flops open like a dead fish, and I snap it closed again and ignore her question. Because no, I have no idea how to effectively guide a horse drawn carriage, and it's one more thing I mentally add to my growing list of shit I need to learn how to do in this world in my free time. Ha! As if I have free time.

"Besides," Lily continues, "I can just leave if it's a problem. Either way, Eve will be fine. She always is."

Lily beams at me and my heart swells at the confidence she has. But I have to admit to a certain amount of nerves. I'm about to meet a dragon face to face. Alone. For reasons unknown. That's not an everyday kinda thing, and I think I'm okay in feeling a bit flustered about it all.

What's the difference between excitement and anxiety? It's hard to say, isn't it? To the body, they are the same. It's only to the mind that they are different. One anticipates a positive outcome in a particular life event, the other anticipates a negative outcome. They are two sides of the same coin.

And so, I do my best to manage my nerves as Lily drives me to the water dragon's palace.

I have so many questions, and I wonder if I'll get any of them answered. We still don't know why they dropped the case against Liam, or what Cole did or said. I'm still waiting for the other shoe to drop. Will this be it? Will today be the day?

Ava'Kara walks down from her throne when we enter, and she doesn't even wait for the standard bows and curtseys. She takes me by the arm and guides me behind her throne into the water that I first saw her emerge from in her dragon form.

Using her powers, she creates a vortex that surrounds us, pulling us to the surface. Ava'Kara is about to use her water manipulation to allow me to breathe, but I beat her to it, channeling my own power to create an air pocket around me.

She raises an eyebrow. "I see you've come into your power. Good. That will make this all go much more smoothly."

"Make what go more smoothly?" I ask, feeling like a parrot.

She studies me with her large blue reptilian eyes. "I need a favor from you. A quite extraordinary one."

"What kind of favor?" I ask, suddenly more nervous than ever, my flash pinging like a winning slot machine in Vegas.

"The kind only you can provide."

We reach a platform made of the largest seashells I've ever seen, and Ava'Kara transforms into her dragon form, her sapphire scales like jewels flashing against the colorful sky.

"Get on," she says.

"You...you want me to ride on your back?" I ask, incredulous.

"It's the fastest way, and we haven't much time. Now!"

Not wanting to argue, but also very much wanting to argue, I ignore my own survival instincts and climb awkwardly onto her back.

She takes off into the sky, and I feel as if I'm being pulled through a wind tunnel.

"Use your air magic," she says loud enough for me to hear her.

I could kick myself for not thinking of that.

I channel my power and manipulate the air around me until it's comfortable. Smiling, I clutch her back and study the scenery below.

It doesn't take long for me to realize we are heading to the edge of the world, where the wall of Dragon's Breath prevents anyone from traveling farther.

Ava'Kara lands us near Kaya the dryad's tree, and I slide off, my legs trembling.

In the center of the grove is the dragon egg, shimmering and pulsing, and there's a crack running down its side. We are alone here, though I can feel the presences of the dryads within their trees.

"It was returned to me," Ava'Kara says, staying in her dragon form. "We know not by whom, but it does not matter. My heir is home, and she is being born as we speak."

Holy shit. Am I about to witness the birth of a dragon?

Yes. Yes, I am.

Because at that moment, the first little dragon claw cuts through the mucous and shell and pokes out, and Ava'Kara makes a strange clucking sound and moves toward her child.

I don't know how long we stand there, but slowly the baby dragon emerges, scales a lighter shade of blue from her mother's, eyes so large they look almost animated, and that newborn innocence that all babies have.

Once she's shed her shell, she takes a few clumsy steps towards her mother, then falls, hiccups, and then quite suddenly turns into a more human-looking baby. She giggles, then turns back into a dragon.

Ava'Kara glances at me. "She'll learn to control that soon enough."

I just nod.

Because holy shit.

The water dragon brings her baby to her, and they snuggle as if they have always been together.

"I need you to perform a ceremony," Ava'Kara says after some time.

"What kind?" I ask. I've read about a lot of different kinds of ceremonies, so I'm hoping it's one I'm familiar with.

"A World Expansion Ceremony," she says softly, setting her child down and shifting into her human form to approach me. "It will require all of the elements, which is why you are the only one who can do it."

"I've never heard of it," I say.

"Because it is the Council of Dragons' most closely guarded secret. Many have paid a steep price for even possessing a fraction of the knowledge I'm about to impart on you tonight," she says.

I think of Lester, rotting in prison because his family knew secrets and lies. And I'm reminded what he said about me, as well. Maybe his ramblings weren't so crazy after all.

"Why is it such a secret?" I ask, my throat dry. I know I'm about to hear something I very much do not want to hear. I feel the fear before I even know why.

"Because it involves the death of a dragon to perform," she says, and I gasp, stepping back.

"You want me to kill a...dragon?" I can't. I cannot.

"I want you to sacrifice me," she says stepping forward.

"You want to kill yourself? Why?" I should start a support group. Nearly every paranormal I've met has serious mental health issues. And for the first time I wonder if there is any kind of mental health services in this world, but I realize this is really not the time and my mind is dissociating from what is happening because I am utterly freaked out.

Eve, note to self, think about all this other shit later. A dragon just asked you to kill her.

"Why?" I ask. It's all I can think to say.

"For too long, we have flown over this world, dictating its rules, running the lives of those in our care, hoarding our own wealth and power. And now our world is crumbling. We are overpopulated and not large enough to manage the growing magical community. Someone has to step forward, and I now have an heir to carry on my element. Only I can do this."

"I don't understand," I say.

"With your powers and my sacrifice, this world will expand, and self-renew, growing as it needs in order to accommodate all of us, present and future. It's this, or so many of us die or live in slums. I can't be the one to condemn my people to that fate." She reaches for my hands and holds them, and I feel her emotions. She is desperate for me to say yes and is very much at peace with her decision. It is the only way to save the people. To save this world.

"Will you help me, Eve?"

My throat is too choked up to speak, so I just nod, glancing over at the baby dragon. She'll never know her mother.

Ava'Kara sees me looking at the baby and sighs. "It is hard to leave her, but she will be raised by someone I trust more than anyone."

The water dragon's face lights up as she glances over my shoulder and I turn around and see Lyx, the Light Dragon walking towards us, arms open. "Sister."

The two dragon queens hug.

"Take care of her for me," Ava'Kara says to Lyx.

Lyx kisses Kara's cheek. "Like she is my own."

Further back, all of the Light Dragon's people stand *en masse*, waiting quietly.

What are they waiting for? I have no idea what will happen.

"Is it safe for them to be here?" I ask.

Ava'Kara nods. "You will expend so much power to me, there will be none left to go anywhere else."

She glances at her sister, who gives her a look. Kara sighs. "There's something I need to tell you," she says.

"Okay… "

Lyx nudges Kara who sighs again. "Performing this ceremony might drain you."

I shrug. "I'll plan on getting extra rest until it all comes back."

Ava'Kara frowns. "Permanently. It might drain you permanently. You might lose all your powers. I don't know. I…we…thought you should know the risks before you agree."

I won't lie. This gives me pause. I could end up stripped of powers I just got? Powers I still don't know the full potential of. Am I willing to give all this up?

I know the answer the moment I think the question. Of course, I am. How could I not be? I may not be all light, but I have to live by a code of some kind. And I can't hoard power if it means so many others suffer.

I nod and the water dragon lets out a breath, then smiles. "You are braver and more generous than I expected, Eve Oliver."

The baby dragon turns back into a child, and Ava'Kara holds her daughter, kissing her head, then passes her to Lyx while she shifts back into her dragon form and positions herself in front of the wall of Dragon's Breath.

"It's very simple," she says. "Channel all the elements and pour them through your hands and into me while chanting *terry autumn usque ad terram.* Of earth, to earth."

I repeat the words in my head then nod and close my eyes. My power is there. It has returned in full form, and I have a feeling I will need every drop.

Hands held out, facing the water dragon, I begin to chant the words and funnel all of my power at the same time through my palms.

The wind whips around us.

A bush catches fire and burns.

The earth rips apart, leaving gashes around my feet.

Water falls from the sky, soaking me to the bone.

Still I chant.

Still the magic flows.

Golden light builds around me, mixed with dark tendrils of smoke. It all surrounds Ava'Kara, who glows a translucent blue, like waves in the ocean.

My knees buckle under me and I land hard on the ground, but I don't stop the ceremony.

Tears stream down my face.

Fire boils under skin.

I'm being drained, as surely as if a vampire was

drinking the last drops of my blood.

My vision flicks in and out.

I can't hear anything over the storm wreaking havoc around me and within me.

And then, there's a great blast that knocks me flat on my face.

Everything goes quiet. Still. And I glance up and see that Ava'Kara is gone. Disappeared entirely.

A low murmur of voices begins behind me, and then the earth under us shifts, and the wall of Dragon's Breath begins to drift away like smoke until we are all staring at a lush new land that goes on as far as the eye can see. Grass green as emeralds, rolling hills, piney forests, the sound of the ocean in the distance. It's paradise.

Lyx wipes a tear form her eyes, holds the baby close to her chest, and nods at me, then steps forward, leading her people into the promised land.

I lay on the ground for I don't know how long—too exhausted and sore to even move—before I hear a familiar voice.

"I got a note to find you here. What happened?" Lily looks around, her face full of shock.

I clutch her arm for strength as I pull myself up. "Let's just go home. I'll explain on the way."

Kaya comes over to us and leans in to hug Lily and whisper something in her ear. They kiss and then Lily guides me to the carriage.

I pass out on the way home and Lily has to actually carry me inside. The dryad is stronger than she looks.

And my mind still hasn't processed all that just happened.

Liam, Sebastian, Derek, and Elijah are all drinking

hard liquor in the study and turn to us when Lily arrives with me in her arms.

Sebastian reaches me first in three long steps, his arms propping me up as Lily releases me to him.

I smile up at him and laugh in a slightly maniacal and exhausted kind of way. "I watched a baby dragon hatch, and then I killed her mother and helped create a new extension to this world with my powers."

The room falls quiet, and the brothers exchange glances.

Elijah looks ready to burst with questions, and I can see him itching to write everything down. But I shake my head. "I need sleep. Food. Wine. I don't know. But definitely quiet. I love you all, and I'll explain everything tomorrow."

My eyelids are hard to keep open, and I step away from Sebastian, but have a hard time steadying myself. Then I feel someone help me, and I'm about to refuse it—because I really do want to be alone for a while—when I realize...it's a ghost. I can't see it, but I can feel it like it's solid.

I tentatively place a little more weight on it, and it shifts to offer more support, walking like this all the way to my room.

When it deposits me into my bed, it stokes the fire, opens a window for fresh air and is about to leave.

"Thank you," I say. "For all your do. Thank you. I will always help maintain your graves, and if you ever can show me where yours is and what your name is, I'll add it to your tombstone."

A gentle breeze blows through me, like a tender caress, and I smile as the door closes and I know I'm finally alone. I flop back onto my pillow, Moon purring at my side, and feel the crinkle of paper under my head.

I reach for it and stare at the script. I've never seen Cole's writing, but I know this is from him. My heart constricts as I open it. Inside the envelope is my onyx ring and a note.

My dearest Eve,

You will likely not believe me, and I wouldn't blame you at all, but not everything I said and did was a lie. You weren't a lie. I promise you that.

My brothers deserved what they got, and I think they know it, too.

But you didn't. You were a casualty of a war that wasn't your own, and for that I will always be deeply sorry.

I'm returning your ring, in hopes you will keep wearing it. It fell off that night.

I didn't get a chance to tell you this, but the ring is a protection ring. That wasn't a lie. I made it with my own powers, which means it even protects you from me. I never wanted you to be caught in something that could harm you. But I failed to consider the emotional cost of what I've done.

It has been too long since I have had any emotion but anger.

But you made me feel something more. Something true and deep and everlasting, even if I never see you again.

I returned the egg. I assume you know that by now.

And I know what you are. I always have.

I still believe you and I are stronger together.

If you ever change your mind, I'll know, and I'll be here.

. . .

JE T'AIME,
   Cole Night

A TEAR FALLS from my cheek onto the paper, casting an inky smear over his signature. I set it aside, but clutch the ring in my palm, then I stand and walk to the balcony and gaze into the distance.

"Oh, Cole," I say into the wind. "How could I ever live with you?" I ask, not expecting an answer. "But how will I ever live without you?"

Already my heart is breaking. I feel like I lost both my brother and Cole in a single night.

I hold the ring to my heart, letting a sob break loose from my throat. I let the tears come, let the emotions wash over me. I give myself permission to feel pain. To feel grief. To not expect happiness for at least a few moments.

We place such a premium on happiness that we deny the reality of our own existence in seeking it. We devalue pain in all its forms, not realizing that the pain can teach us so much more than the joy. The joy is our reward for the lessons learned through pain. We wouldn't have the joy without it.

So, I embrace my own pain and I cry until there are no more tears.

I cry for Cole. For Adam. For myself. For this family that is broken and may never truly be mended.

I cry for Ava'Kara, who was the first of the dragons with the courage to sacrifice herself to save this world.

Even the Beggar Queen chose a path that kept her alive. Sure, she drained her magic to help, but she didn't make the ultimate sacrifice and she could have. In the end, it was Ava'Kara. Maybe that was because the water dragon had an heir, but that doesn't make her sacrifice any less noble. I wear her ring on my right hand now, at her request before she died.

Someday I will give it to her daughter, when she is ready.

I open my palm and study the other ring recently given to me. Now that I know what I'm looking for, I can feel Cole's energy in the stone, pulsing at the same frequency that he does. It sends warmth through my body when I slip it on my finger, and I know the moment I do that I won't be taking it off again.

Someday, I have hope that Cole will come home for good. That this family will be complete.

Until then, I will be the best mother to Alina I can, and the best partner to other brothers. I will hold us together and help make us stronger.

There's a knock at the door, and a platter of food flies in seemingly of its own accord.

One of the ghosts has brought me food and wine and water, as requested. I smile.

And when I look down at my plate, I realize my vegetables spell something.

Mable.

A name.

"Are you Mable?"

The fire flares, and I know it's not my doing. I have nothing left in my magical reserves. "I take that as a yes. I'm Eve. It's such a pleasure to meet you."

Once Mable leaves, I head to the bathroom to ready myself for bed.

When I come out, I nearly shit myself in shock.

Standing in my bedroom by the fire is the woman I've been seeing flashes of since my interview for the Night Firm.

Tall, ebony skin with silver hair and large luminous silver eyes. And a silver horn sticking out of her forehead.

She looks like the human-ish version of a black unicorn.

"Eve Oliver, I would say it's about time, but I know this must be quite the shock. But do understand, I have been waiting for one of the Fates to release me from my binding for millennia. I just never expected until recently that it would be you." She walks over to me and holds up my arms, studying me. "And look at you. You really have returned."

"What are you talking about?" I ask.

She cocks her head. "I'm talking about you, Eve Oliver. The Maiden Fate has finally returned. In you."

THE SAGA CONTINUES

**Want to know what happens next? Grab I AM THE NIGHT, book 3 of THE NIGHT FIRM.

Want to get I Am the Night, and all our books, before anyone else? Plus free music and weekly interactive flash fiction? Join our patreon at patreon.com/KarpovKinrade

Enjoy this series with the fantasy soundtrack we composed for it. Grab I AM THE WILD music on iTunes, Apple Music, Spotify, Amazon, Google Play and more.

AFTERWORD

NOTE FROM THE AUTHOR

When I started I Am the Wild, I was grieving the loss of my own brother to suicide. When I wrote I Am the Storm, I realized grief comes in waves. So too does healing. And acceptance. And more grief. Healing happens in layers, and it's complex. More complex than I could include in these books. But as you read this series, know that it comes from a deep place within me. A place of pain and sadness and hope and love and light and darkness. We all have it all within us. We are all bound by the elements of this life. It is my one hope that in addition to entertaining you, this series also inspires you to hold onto hope. To embrace all the parts of yourself, including your shadows. And to live fully. To love deeply, even when it hurts. To not be scared of pain.

Don't give up. You're not alone.

~Lux

ACKNOWLEDGMENTS

THANK YOUS...

Thanks to Joe for all the editing and for going above and beyond in all the ways! To Lind for cracking the whip, proofing, encouraging and being the most amazing friend. And Bam for all the awesome graphics and brainstorming and help launching this new series.

Special love to the KK Coven for always being our tribe.

We'd especially like to thank all those who helped hunt down poems to use for the chapter heads:

Brittany Anne, Melinda Kahler, Kayla Myers, Makalae Stephens, Kaitlin Rafalski, Rachel Ziemann, Allison Woerner, Leticia Velasquez, Shelah Kai, Kimberley Tuong, Bunny Summerland, Heavan Cook, Darla Stone, Shannon Johnson Mastin, Jennifer Borak

And finally, to our patrons. We love you all! Every tier, every single one of you is everything.

Love,
Lux & D

ABOUT THE AUTHOR

Karpov Kinrade is the pen name for the husband and wife writing duo of USA TODAY bestselling, award-winning authors Lux Karpov-Kinrade and Dmytry Karpov-Kinrade.

Together, they live in Ukiah, California and write fantasy and science fiction novels and screenplays, make music and direct movies.

Look for more from Karpov Kinrade in *The Night Firm*, *Vampire Girl*, *Of Dreams and Dragons*, *Nightfall*

Academy and *Paranormal Spy Academy*. If you're looking for their suspense and romance titles, you'll now find those under Alex Lux.

They live with their three teens who share a genius for all things creative, and seven cats who think they rule the world (spoiler, they do.)

Want their books and music before anyone else and also enjoy weekly interactive flash fiction? Join them on Patreon at Patreon.com/karpovkinrade

Find them online at KarpovKinrade.com

On Facebook /KarpovKinrade

On Twitter @KarpovKinrade

And subscribe to their newsletter at ReadKK.com for special deals and up-to-date notice of new launches.

~~~~~

If you enjoyed this book, consider supporting the author by leaving a review wherever you purchased this book. Thank you.

Get the soundtrack for I AM THE WILD, OF DREAMS AND DRAGONS and MOONSTONE ACADEMY wherever music can be found.

Nightfall Academy

Court of Nightfall

Weeper of Blood

House of Ravens

Night of Nyx

Song of Kai

Daughter of Strife

Paranormal Spy Academy (complete academy sci fi thriller romance)

Forbidden Mind

Forbidden Fire

Forbidden Life

Our ALEX LUX BOOKS!

The Seduced Saga (paranormal romance with suspense)

Seduced by Innocence

Seduced by Pain

Seduced by Power

Seduced by Lies

Seduced by Darkness

The Call Me Cat Trilogy (romantic suspense)

Call Me Cat

Leave Me Love

Tell Me True

(Standalone romcon with crossover characters)

Hitched

Whipped

Kiss Me in Paris (A standalone romance)

Our Children's Fantasy collection under Kimberly Kinrade

Printed in Great Britain
by Amazon